Falling for Kate

Grandma
Happy Holiday
♡ u
Jody.

An Angel's Lake Novella

JODY HOLFORD

LOS ANGELES, CALIFORNIA

Copyright © 2016 by Jody Holford

All rights reserved. No part of this publication may be reproduced, distributed or transmitted in any form or by any means, including photocopying, recording, or other electronic or mechanical methods, without the prior written permission of the publisher, except in the case of brief quotations embodied in critical reviews and certain other noncommercial uses permitted by copyright law. For permission requests, write to the publisher below.

Penner Publishing
P.O. Box 57914
Los Angeles, California
www.pennerpublishing.com

Publisher's Note: This is a work of fiction. Names, characters, places, and incidents are a product of the author's imagination. Locales and public names are sometimes used for atmospheric purposes. Any resemblance to actual people, living or dead, or to businesses, companies, events, institutions, or locales is completely coincidental.

Falling for Kate/ Jody Holford -- 1st ed.
ISBN 978-1-944179-44-1

Interior Design and Formatting by:
www.emtippettsbookdesigns.com

Also by
JODY HOLFORD

Falling for Home
Damaged
Caught Looking

"*You may not always end up where you thought you were going. But you will always end up where you are meant to be.*"

~unknown

Praise for
Falling for Kate

"I enjoyed every minute of Kate finding where she belongs, a sweet story full of heart and humor ♡"

—*Cole Robitaille*

"There are so many things I loved about Kate and Elliott's story, but my favorite thing about it was how effortless their love was for each other."

—*Tanya Baikie (I ♡ Books)*

"If you take all the words like passionate, loving, nurturing, forgiving etc and wrapped it up in the intense emotion that radiates off of Kate and Elliott in their journey to find and help each other get to their happy place and become a loving already made family, that would be how I would describe Falling for Kate."

—*Julie Hillier, Reader*

Chapter One

Kate Aarons wanted her mom. Or one of her sisters. Or a magic wand. The customer service agent smiled like she could solve all of Kate's problems.

"There's a flight leaving for Duluth, Minnesota at three p.m. tomorrow," the woman said.

Kate's smile probably looked more like someone was poking her in the back with a sharpened stick. "Is there any flight that can get me in or around, just somewhere closer to, Angel's Lake tonight? Please?"

"She said tomorrow, lady. Take it or leave it," the guy behind her grumbled.

Kate whirled, gripping the strap of her Louis Vuitton carry-on like a lifeline. The imposingly tall man stood too close for Kate's comfort—or for common courtesy—and the last of her patience vanished.

Kate pointed to the red line on the floor. "See that line? It's where the next customer waits their turn. You should be behind it."

She was certain the oh-no-you-didn't smile on her face was at odds with the tone of her voice, but he stepped back, eyebrows arched, and shrugged. Living in New York for two years had taught her how to navigate more than the fashion industry.

Turning back to the attendant, Kate let out a sigh. "Okay. Thank you. I'm going to think about it."

"Of course. Sorry it's not sooner," the attendant said.

Kate nodded and walked away from the counter. She was choosing to go home. It wasn't failure if it was a choice. New York had worn her down. When people talked about the city never sleeping, they failed to mention that the people didn't either. Not if they wanted to get ahead, or anywhere, in an industry with a revolving door and a demand for perfection. Kate wanted home. Now, preferably. And not just because it would put her a plane ride away from the biggest mistake of her almost-twenty-five years—one who had conveniently forgotten to mention he had a wife.

She was going home because Angel's Lake was more than a place. It was the only place where she knew who she was and how she fit. Now if she could just get there.

An announcement sounded over the speakers, urging passengers to head to their departure gate. *Must be nice.* Her flight from New York had made an unexpected landing in Wisconsin due to engine troubles that Kate didn't want to think too much about. Particularly since she still had to get on another plane. The airport was doing its best to be accommodating, and she now had a travel voucher for anywhere her airline flew, but still, she wanted to get home. She could wait. It wasn't a big deal. But she really didn't want to.

Going home had been in the back of her mind for months. Once she'd gotten on the plane this morning, the need to *be home* had consumed her, swallowed her up in one painful gulp until she almost ached.

Kate scanned the signs, looking for a place to get coffee. Her phone buzzed in her pocket and she pulled it out as she started toward a café. The sight of her sister Lucy's name on the screen made her heart pinch. She smothered the worry that Lucy, who was the reason she'd been able to be a part of New York's fashion world, would be upset. *Please don't be disappointed Luce.*

Sliding her finger across the screen, she read Lucy's text.

Lucy: Did you get a flight? I have an idea.

Oh no. Kate wasn't sure she wanted to know Lucy's plan. Despite having been, as their older sister Char liked to tease, domesticated after happily settling into a life with her husband and daughter in Angel's Lake, Lucy's spirit was still more adventurous than Kate's. It was with some well-placed trepidation that Kate responded.

Kate: No flights until tomorrow. I hate airports. What's your idea? I'm not hitchhiking.

The reply was nearly instantaneous, which told Kate she'd already been in the midst of texting.

Lucy: Alex told me Elliot had to get the girls in Reedsburg. That's about an hour from Dane County Airport. That's where you are right? He left early yesterday and stayed the night. They're heading back and if you can get there, you can ride with him.

Kate's stomach dipped—in a good way. *Elliot.* Elliot Peters was one of her brother-in-law's officers. He looked more like a raven-haired, sun-kissed surfer than he did a cop. Laidback and sweet, he had adorable twin daughters and an ex who often made his life difficult.

Kate had had a crush on him before she'd left for New York. Most women with a pulse had a crush on Elliot. Especially when he was around his daughters. In addition to the hot factor, the kind and funny factors, or the sexy cop factor, he was a trusted friend and not far away.

Kate: Why the hell are the girls in Wisconsin and since when?

Kate sidestepped a couple of teens sprawled out on the floor, heads resting on their large backpacks. Her stomach growled, and she looked around to see what she could grab. Her phone whistled with her sister's incoming text.

Lucy: Crazy ex has a sister there she thought she could live off of. Sis doesn't want kids there. E finally doing a hard push for full custody. This should seal it. Yes or no? Can I text him? Tell him to wait for you? Can you get somewhere to meet him?

God. As if it wasn't bizarre enough that Gina hadn't appreciated having Elliot as hers, she was also a shit mom to two of the sweetest children ever. All three of them deserved better. *A thought for another time.*

Kate: Yes. Tell me where. I'll go find a cab.

Lucy texted an address a few minutes later. Elliot texted approximately ten minutes later as Kate was climbing into a taxi.

Elliot: You on your way?

She sent a quick reply after giving the cabbie the address. Elliot's response made her smile.

Elliot: Grace and Beth are going to make you wish

you'd waited for the next flight. I'll be glad to have backup.

Kate pictured Elliot and his two dark-haired little girls who had his gorgeous skin tone, his happy smile, and rich, stare-worthy eyes, so brown they were nearly black.

> **Kate: LOL. I won't tell anyone you needed it for those two sweet little girls**

> **Elliot: I am going to enjoy watching you eat those words. I love them, but they do not love car rides. You're stuck now, Aarons.**

> **Kate: Technically, I could turn around and wait for the flight**

As if she'd give up the chance to spend seven hours in a vehicle with Elliot. Or get home as quick as possible. That was the main reason she reminded herself. Because she was certainly in no position to start up anything with anyone. Let alone Elliot, who had enough drama in his life.

> **Elliot: Sure. You do that and I'll just try to console my sweet babies who are so excited you're joining us.**

Low blow. But she chuckled and imagined the smile widening on his face. It was a really good face. She'd put it out of her mind when she'd left for New York to do an internship at a top fashion house. Then of course, another face had gotten in the way and distracted her. Not that dating Elliot was an option. They were only friends. Kate had so many things to sort through—going home, finding a space to lease, spending time with her family—she didn't have time for any activities involving her heart or her body. Besides, Alex, Lucy's husband, would lose his mind. He definitely considered Kate a little sister and thus saw her as untouchable. And he was Elliot's boss.

Best to leave that stone forever unturned.

> **Lucy: Are you in a cab yet? Are you almost there? When will you be home? Hurry up.**

Kate laughed. It felt good to be wanted. Missed.

> **Lucy: Get home now and you can wrap my gifts for me.**

The cab swerved slightly, catching Kate off guard as she rolled her eyes at her sister's text. Patience and subtlety weren't Lucy's strong suits.

"Sorry about that," the cabbie said, putting up a hand. "Guy cut me off."

Kate nodded. "No worries." She checked the tightness of her seat belt and pushed her shoulders against the seat. *This guy should be a New York cabbie.*

> **Elliot: Hey. I was just teasing.**

> **Kate: I know. Was going to give sarcastic reply but cabbie thinks he's on the race circuit.**

> **Kate: Luce, breathe. I'll be there when I get there. And I bet your presents will be waiting. Luv u.**

Her sister sent a long string of smiley faces and hearts, making Kate grin. Then she sent a gorgeous selfie of her and Emma, Lucy and Alex's almost two-year-old. Her heart pinched tightly. Home was exactly where she wanted to be.

Kate's phone buzzed throughout the entire drive, as she sent playful, innocent texts back and forth with Elliot to pass the time. She didn't watch through the window to take in what she could of Wisconsin because it just didn't matter. All she wanted was the view of Angel's Lake.

Snow would be covering everything, making the town sparkle like a sheet of glass. The lake would be frozen, and the plows would be trudging through the streets. Her dad would have already stocked up on salt to make sure none of his girls slipped on their way up icy front steps.

There'd been no snow or ice when she'd gotten hurt in New York. It was an invisible pain, right in the center of her heart. Not really heartbreak, but more heart-shame at being so gullible. Going home, being with her family would hopefully fill the hole that burned there, reminding her how stupid she'd been. How naïve. Never again. She wouldn't be duped by another man. And for now, Kate wasn't even thinking of a man. Or men. She had priorities, including her career and establishing herself. No room for men in that plan.

Now, if she could just remind herself of that once she was in cramped quarters with Sexy Elliot Peters.

Chapter Two

Elliot felt like he was playing that game the girls loved where they moved their hand up and down in front of their face, changing their expressions from happy to sad. Only his was going from amused to pissed off. Amused. Pissed. Kate was making him smile, and Gina was pissing him off. He wasn't even going to respond to her last text, asking if he was mad. *Jesus.* It was like high school with her.

"Daddy, can I have more hot chocolate?" Beth asked, coming to stand in front of him.

His hands were hanging between his knees, holding his phone as he stared at Kate's latest text. Looking up into his daughter's eyes, he felt the same tug he always did. He loved both of them so much it overshadowed his constant irritation with their mother.

"No, sweet pea. Don't want you to feel sick in the car," he said.

Gracie came back from the bathroom. If people looked really closely, they noticed the small beauty mark next to Beth's lip and used that tiny difference to tell them apart. Now that they weren't babies and had distinct personalities, Elliot saw distinctions in the way they talked, stood, and even laughed. But he'd trained himself to pay attention to those subtleties.

"When's Kate gonna be here?" Grace asked.

"Can I play with your phone?" Beth asked at the same time.

"It's my turn to play with it," Grace chimed in.

Elliot shook his head and rubbed at his temples where a headache was beginning to spread like a crack in the earth.

"No more hot chocolate, no phone, Kate will be here soon. Now both of you sit down and color or draw, okay? Please."

Maybe it was his tone or maybe his seven-year-olds were both as tired as he was, but they sat down with the coloring books he'd grabbed them at the dollar store and chatted quietly with each other.

He was thinking about topping up his coffee for the first part of the drive when he saw Kate get out of a taxi. The café windows were painted with happy Christmas scenes: elves, toys, and reindeer. He could see the full length of Kate's body, bundled in a long wool coat, between two of the hand-drawn presents. *Yeah, she's a present all right. One he'd love to unwrap one slow piece at a time. And then Alex can kick your ass to hell and back again.*

She laughed at something the driver said and waved. The Aarons sisters were a sight to behold. Sexy, sweet, and smart—all three of them. Alex was married to Lucy, and the oldest sister was married to Luke, who Elliot played cards and pool with. Char and Luke had two daughters, one of whom was close to Grace and Beth's age. They all played together now and again.

Elliot was a fan of Kate's whole family, but she'd always stood out to him. She had a sultry voice that felt like fingertips grazing over his skin and when she spoke to someone, her eyes stayed fastened on theirs, like she was fully invested, regardless of the conversation. Like she cared.

As she walked into the café, he had an "if only" thought. If only he'd seen who Gina really was before she'd told him she was pregnant. If only he was in a place to make Kate Aarons *his*.

Beth giggled and his gaze shifted to his girls. Gina was a pain in the ass, but he wouldn't trade them for anything. Not even Kate. Besides, Gina had shown him happily ever after had a shelf life when the reality of living together and raising kids encroached.

"Is this seat taken?" Kate asked the girls.

The squealing pierced his ears like needles, and Elliot winced, even as he tried to smile. Kate laughed and bent down to hug his girls. They were excited to see her, sure, but mostly, they wanted to get home and jump into all things Christmas. Now that Kate had arrived, they could get going. Elliot had learned the hard way: waiting was not considered fun in the eyes of his girls.

The girls asked her a dozen questions, not even waiting for a response while Kate tried her best to answer them, shooting him a gut-clenching grin over Gracie's head.

"Do you like country music? Daddy hates it."

"Can you sit in the back with me?"

"How come you're not on a plane?"

"We got hot chocolate. Are you getting some? Daddy, can we get doughnuts?"

"Do you got snacks?"

"Daddy said it's supposed to snow more."

Elliot stood and grabbed Kate's forearm, pulling her out of his girls' clutches. "All right, let her breathe you two. And Beth, it's: do you *have* snacks. Come here, Aarons."

And even though pulling her close was a stupid thing to do, when she gave him an all-out, no-holds-barred, squeeze-him-tight embrace, he was glad he did. Partially because she was his friend, partially because she was really fucking hot, and a surprising amount because he really needed a hug. And Kate Aarons gave exceptional hugs.

"You okay?" she whispered.

He pulled back and brushed a stray hair from her cheek. Her eyes watched his and this close, he could see they were a deep, shimmering blue, like water rippling. Unstill but soothing.

"Yeah. Eager to get home. Look at you," he said and did.

If she had on make-up, he couldn't tell. Her skin was flawless but he saw the subtle creases of fatigue and hoped they were just from traveling. Looking at her now, he realized that he'd missed her. Even putting aside the deeply rooted attraction he tried to ignore, Elliot enjoyed being around her as much as, or maybe more than, the rest of her family.

Kate shook her head, sending strands of hair fluttering. "Right, look at me after being on a plane, hanging out in an airport, feeling rumpled and grumpy. Please, look your fill," she said, laughing and releasing him.

The invitation tightened his stomach and he shut down the sensation quickly by taking a step back from her. *Fuck.* What was he doing? She'd been off limits from the minute he'd met her. He was in no place for this shit. Things needed to change for his girls. A steady life with a predictable routine was what he needed to focus on, not hooking up with someone. Or starting a relationship. Certainly not with Kate Aarons, who was one of Angel's Lake's three sweethearts. He was just nursing an old crush, feeling sentimental. Or, maybe he needed to get laid. At one point in his life, this hadn't been a problem. But since Gina and the girls, most of his time was focused on work or being a single dad. Didn't leave much room, or energy, for anything else.

"Daddy, can we go?"

Grace sneezed and Kate "blessed her," pulling a tissue out of her pocket and handing it to her.

"Did you girls use the bathroom? It's a long drive," Kate said.

"We did. Daddy didn't. Do you have to go pee, Daddy?" Beth asked.

Kate muffled her laugher, or tried to, but his face still flamed. He shot Beth a look that she just smiled back at.

With a mockingly stern gaze, Kate said, "You better try. It's a long drive."

He narrowed his eyes at her, and this time she didn't try to hide her giggles. The girls joined in immediately and Elliot rolled his eyes and went to use the bathroom.

It still took another twenty minutes to get the girls loaded and situated. They had their earphones in and the DVD set up to play. He'd stocked snacks, water, Kleenex, and a host of stuffed animals—each with names he was supposed to remember—in between them. By all accounts, they were good to go.

"You want me to drive for a bit?" Kate asked as he loaded her bag into the back.

"Nah. Maybe later. You good? Alex said you might stay longer than Christmas," Elliot said.

He couldn't imagine living in New York, but Kate had been pumped to move there a couple of years ago and had been full of stories during her visits home. The icy breeze blew through them and she hunched her shoulders.

"I'm good. Time to come home is all."

He kept staring even though she looked down at her feet. Ignoring his own warnings about keeping some distance, he reached out and tipped her chin up with his fingers.

"Time to come home…for Christmas you mean, right? Angel's Lake is hardly the fashion capital of Minnesota."

Kate smiled, but it was only a shadow of the real thing. "Actually," she started then paused. Straightening her shoulders as if she was steeling herself against a storm, she continued, "for good. And don't give me your cop eyes, mister. Maybe it's not the fashion capital, but it could do with a decent dress shop. I'm going to make that happen."

He didn't know what to do with the knowledge that Kate Aarons was coming home to stay. Elliot shoved his hands in his pockets and shook his head, wishing her motivated attitude didn't make her even sexier.

"You three were born with more drive and energy than most of our town put together."

Kate laughed, a hint of her genuine, heart-felt laugh. "We'll see how it pans out. For now, I need to get home, let my mother feel like she's healing my chakras or whatever the focus of her newest book is, and find a place to live. Because as much as I want to go home, I do *not* want to move back in with my mom and dad."

Elliot's thoughts tumbled over that knowledge: She needed somewhere to stay and he needed someone to watch the girls while he was at work. *Not a good idea.*

"Daddy! Are we going?" Beth yelled through the partially rolled-down window.

Kate grinned. "Better get on the road. They sleep for any of it?"

"No such luck, Aarons. But the DVD will keep them busy for a bit before they make us do a Disney sing-a-long."

She didn't look scared. But she'd see. Only so much of the *Frozen* soundtrack any adult could take.

Chapter Three

The 94 North was fairly smooth sailing, and the girls had settled into their movie easily enough, singing along with the songs. Kate played around with his iPhone, switching the music before any song had a chance to end.

Elliot glanced at her as a new song came through the speakers. "Do you just not like endings?"

Kate looked over, her brows drawn together. "What?"

He pointed to the iPhone. "You haven't let one song finish."

"They are finished. You don't need to hear the last of it because it's just the singer wrapping up the chorus for the final time. It's over."

"It's not over until the song ends."

"You've heard all the lyrics, the music is dying out. It's over."

"Weirdo. You need to take things all the way to the finish line, Aarons."

She smiled at him and switched his phone for hers. A Christmas song came through the speakers. He groaned, knowing it was payback.

"Don't worry, *Peters*, I'll let it go all the way to the end."

They'd settled into a comfortable drive, her telling him about interning, crazy models, and Lucy's good friend, Kael, whom Kate had interned for. She didn't mention much of a social life or what it was that brought her home. He didn't think it was his place to ask, though he was definitely curious. *Curiosity killed the cat and Alex will fucking skin you like one if you don't shut this down.*

Kate turned and checked on the girls, who were still quiet. Then he felt her eyes on him. He felt her arm close to his and the scent of her shampoo and skin was all he could smell. She leaned toward him a little.

"So, Gina ask you if she could take the girls to Wisconsin?"

His hands tightened on the steering wheel. "Nope. Gina's more of a seek-forgiveness woman. Does what she wants and backpedals after."

"You have a lawyer?"

He shook his head, threw her a quick glance to see her face was as dark as he felt inside. "I need to get on that. This shit has to stop. I want them with me. They won't be going back with her. I've got them now. She wants them, she'll need to move in and that sure as hell isn't happening."

Kate's hand covered his arm, squeezed, then was removed just as quickly. "They should be with you. You're a great dad. They need the stability you can offer them."

He nodded. He knew this, and it was time to stop hoping his ex would get her head out of her ass long enough to think about their daughters more than herself. Since she wouldn't, it was on him to get them settled into a life and routine they could count on. Which meant no time for dating or even entertaining thoughts of taking the woman next to him out for an evening, or more.

"You go to school with any lawyers?" he asked, mostly joking.

"No, but when I was finishing my social work degree, I did a practicum at Family Services and they've got all of those types of contacts. They can connect you with a lawyer who won't kill your budget."

His hands tightened again. He hadn't wanted to do things this way. He'd hoped he and Gina could keep things easy, friendly. She loved their daughters. She was a good woman, underneath the thoughtless acts. Gina didn't think about consequences…or others. She went with what she wanted and how it made *her* feel. It had been fine, mostly, until now. This time, Gina had gone too far. Taking his girls out of the state did not make him feel easy or friendly.

"I'm not broke."

"No. But if she decides to fight this, it could go on for a while. Anyway, they can provide counsel and advice, even if you don't hire them in the end. Something to think about."

Gina had no money to fight anything. It was another tension between them—sometimes he felt like he was paying for three kids.

Elliot nodded again. It was all he thought about. "Your mom must be freaking out that all her girls are home to stay."

He heard her suck in a breath before she replied, "She will be."

"You didn't tell her?"

"No. I wanted to get through Christmas. There will be so much excitement, and I don't want to put a damper on anything. I want to make it through the holidays and spend some time with my nieces and sisters before I dive into explanations and plans."

He couldn't figure out how having her home for good would put a damper on anything. Her family would be thrilled.

"With them?" He glanced at her. She was adjusting her coat, trying to get it off without removing her seatbelt.

"Hmm?"

"You're keeping quiet with them. Can you share with me?"

Kate pulled her arm through and he reached to hold it for her so she could tug on the other side. Her shirt gapped a tiny bit between the buttons. Enough for him to see a glimpse of smooth, creamy skin and a flash of purple satin. *Fuck*. Eyes back on the road, he felt her moving around, his hand still on the end of her sleeve. Finally, she pulled it from his grasp.

"Thanks. Phew. That was the closest I've come to a work out in a long time," she said, laughter lightening her voice.

If the girls weren't in the car or he had any right at all, he'd tell her that even without working out, she was fucking gorgeous. Staying quiet, trying to keep his thoughts on getting them all home safely, despite the snow that was starting to fall, he waited for her to explain. As a cop, he knew silence could be his best friend when it came to getting information from someone. People felt compelled to fill in the quiet.

"I want to start a dress shop."

"You mentioned that."

"I want to do it on my own. Without everyone telling me how it should be, you know? I love my family. They're well-meaning, but going home means pulling everyone in. They'll all have an opinion on where and what and how, and I already have those ideas, so I want to make sure I can get the ball rolling before I tell them. I have the small business loan filled out online. I just need to press send."

She shifted in the seat, setting it back a bit before angling toward him.

"I can't move back home. It'll feel like a step back. It's one thing to come for Christmas but another entirely to move back into my old bedroom and stay. Even for a bit. I don't feel like the same person I was when I left, and I think staying there will make me feel like I should be." She rubbed her hands over her face and gave a not-so-certain laugh. "That sounds ridiculous, doesn't it?"

Elliot shrugged. "I don't think so. Sounds like you moved away, grew up, got the experience you wanted and needed, and made the best decision for yourself. Now you're home and want to start a life on your own terms. It sounds like being an adult."

She nudged him in the shoulder. "Thanks oh wise one. When did you get so smart?"

He chuckled, flashed her a quick grin and winked at her. "I've always been this smart. You were just too blinded by my good looks to dig deeper."

Her face went red like the skin of summer cherries and desire curled in his belly. He'd been joking but the look on her face said she had in fact been very aware of his looks.

Gracie's voice hit a particularly high note in one of the songs, pulling him out of his thoughts. Tightening his hold on the steering wheel, he trained his eyes, and his brain, back on the road.

"Plus, having kids makes you see things differently. Nothing wrong with growing up and getting what you want out of life. That takes drive and determination. And a solid plan."

"It does. Let's just hope mine is solid."

He laughed. "I hope mine is too."

They'd driven a little farther, and the sun was starting to sink into the horizon, ready to give up for the day and let the moon take over. Kate yawned and he thought he heard another yawn coming from the back.

"Daddy," Beth moaned.

Kate turned in her seat and Elliot glanced at the rear view mirror. Gracie was out, but Beth was pale.

"What's wrong, pumpkin?"

"I don't feel so good."

Shit. "What doesn't feel good?"

"My belly."

Kate glanced at him. "She's a little pale." Kate adjusted her belt and reached back. "Can you lean forward, sweetie?" She must have because Kate settled back in her seat and said, "She's warm."

"Daddy," Beth said again, her voice low and mournful. It twisted his gut.

"Okay, Beth. I'll pull over at the next stop. You got a bag back there in case you throw up?"

At this, Beth started to cry, waking Grace. "I don't want to throw up. Throwing up is gross."

"You threw up?" Grace asked, coming fully awake.

Kate loosened her seatbelt again and Elliot switched lanes, heading for the exit up ahead.

"Hey sweetie, can you take a small sip of water?"

Beth shook her head "no" through her tears. He hated when the girls cried. Regardless of the reason, it made him feel helpless, like his hands were tied behind his back with zip strips.

"It's okay, Bethy. You're okay," Grace said.

No matter what—they had each other's backs. Every damn time. Fuck, he really loved his kids.

"Oooh, no," Beth moaned.

Kate undid her seat belt and shuffled around, twisting to reach his daughter. He heard rustling and Grace squealed and then he heard

Beth throwing up.

He took the exit, trying not to be distracted by Kate's very sweet ass, which was practically in his face. Pressing the brake gently, he hoped she didn't go flying. Her voice was soft and sweet; she was taking care of his kid and that was as sexy as the rest of her.

"It's okay, sweetheart. You're okay. Grace, stop crying, honey. She's fine."

Sniffles and tears were the soundtrack to Elliot finding a gas station and finally pulling over. When he did, he got out of the truck, took the bag from Kate's hand, tied it, and pulled his daughter out of her belt and into his arms.

"You okay, sweet pea?"

"Daddy, I'm sweet pea," Grace said from her seat. Yeah, they had each other's backs…until they didn't. And then they would again.

"You're both sweet peas. Beth?"

She nuzzled into him, her small arms going around his neck. "I don't think I'm going to throw up no more, Daddy."

He rubbed her back. "Okay. We'll just take a little break."

"I don't wanna get back in the car, Daddy," Beth said into the crook of his neck.

"We have to get home. We haven't even decorated for Christmas, sweetie. I was waiting for you guys."

"The car makes my belly mad," Beth said, sniffling.

"She threw up four times when Mommy was driving us to Aunt Shelly's," Grace said, getting out of the car too.

Kate came around to the driver's side where he was holding Beth. Grace was holding her hand. Their eyes met, and he easily recognized the flash of anger in Kate's. It was a mirror image of his own.

"Your mom didn't tell me that."

"Mommy said she just needed more practice at long car rides," Grace said.

Elliot squeezed his daughter tight. "Why didn't you tell me the car made you feel yucky?"

Beth leaned back and put her hands to his cheeks, squeezing them a bit. "Because I thought it was practice and it wasn't so bad at first." She rested her forehead against his. It wasn't hot, but it was clammy.

"Why don't Grace and I go grab some fresh waters and I'll see if they have something for her belly?" Kate put a hand on his arm.

Looking down at her, he nodded. "Kate, we might need to stop for the night."

He braced for irritation, at least a touch of it, at having her desire to get home thwarted by his kids. She'd eaten the cost of a plane ticket and a taxi just to drive with him and get home quicker. Instead, she tilted her head and a smile spread across her face, carefree, like a flower blooming one petal at a time.

"That's probably a good idea. I'll ask the clerk if there's anything close by." She touched her finger to Beth's nose. "Sound okay?"

Beth nodded. Grace tugged on her hand and looked up. "Maybe there's a pool."

Kate just laughed, grabbed the bag from Elliot's hand and pulled Grace along with her into the small convenience store attached to the gas station. She chucked the bag into the trash bin, like she dealt with vomiting seven-year-olds every day.

"Sorry, Daddy," Beth whispered.

His heart squeezed like a fist. Leaning in to nuzzle her, he kissed her cheek, making her giggle. "Don't say sorry. You okay to settle back in for a few minutes? I'm sure there's something close by."

She nodded and he helped her put her seat belt on. He was in his seat when Grace and Kate came back out with a plastic bag of snacks and drinks. She helped Grace get settled and then got in beside him.

"Not only is there a Best Western with an indoor pool down the street, but I also bought some ginger ale. When I was little, my mom always gave it to me and my sisters. Made my tummy feel better," Kate said, her body angled toward the girls.

Turning back, Kate smiled at him and the fist around his heart tightened again, but in an entirely different way. In a way that said, *she's a natural with your girls.* He quashed the thought and gestured to her with his chin. "Seat belt, Aarons."

She gave him a full-mouthed grin. "Do you call me that because you can't remember which of the sisters I am?"

He wished like hell he could think of her the way he thought of the other two. But his heart and body refused to cooperate; neither realized how much he didn't need another complication. And though she made him laugh and turned him on, the Aarons girls weren't the kind of women to just have a fling, regardless of their adventurous spirits. Or maybe they were…how would he know? What he was sure of, was if he were to find out that Kate was up for a short-term hook up, her father and brother-in-law would probably shine up a couple of shotguns. Elliot was barely wrapping his head around committing his life to his daughters. There wasn't enough of him left to give Kate the kind of relationship she deserved. Not that she was asking.

His hand was on the gearshift and he waited until her eyes fastened back on his. "I know exactly which one you are. Always have, Kate."

Her eyes widened and her lips parted. He called her Aarons because he liked the way her name sounded on his lips, perhaps too much. And he liked the way the little "O" formed on her mouth when he said it.

Clenching his jaw, he gave his head a small shake. *Enough.* His girls needed some rest and then he'd get them all home so they could settle into something that resembled a normal life. Until their mother swept in and tried to shake it up again.

Chapter Four

Kate turned to her other side on the scratchy sheets. It didn't make the mattress any more comfortable so she rolled to her back, staring into the darkness. If she focused, she could smell the subtle trace of Elliot's cologne, which was a far better smell than the staleness of the comforter she was lying under. After the girls had bathed, Beth ate some crackers, and both girls had ginger ale, they'd settled onto the beds to watch the Disney channel.

Elliot had texted Alex to say he'd be delayed and back at work the day after tomorrow. Kate had turned off the lights a while ago but she couldn't sleep. Instead, she was listening to the sound of two adorable girls snoring and trying to measure Elliot's breaths, wondering if they signified sleep. He and the girls took the bed closest to the bathroom, just in case, but getting out of the car seemed to settle Beth's stomach. Between her mother's impromptu trip and Elliot's desire to have them home, they needed the break and Kate was happy to stop for the night if it helped Beth. The urgency to get home had faded a bit in Elliot's presence.

Kate felt badly for Elliot and the girls. The tug of war that came with shared custody had to be hard on all parties involved. She was lucky to have her parents, who'd weathered their own storms, but came through them together. Kate had gone through most of her life with the kind of blissful-take-no-notice ignorance that came to those who'd never had it any other way.

Her family was all about love and protection. Honesty and caring and a sometimes, too much oversharing. They made mistakes, all of them. They'd hurt each other—they were human and all had their share of faults—but underneath, they wanted what was best for each other.

In Kate's mind, Gina thought too much about what she wanted—like getting to her sister's house—regardless of what that meant for her girls, like upset tummies. Kate hated seeing what Gina did to Elliot. He was the safety net, the one who picked up the pieces when the consequences of Gina's irresponsibility emerged.

Kate was about to get up, tiptoe to the mini fridge, and grab a bottle of water when she heard a distinctive, "Oomph," followed by a low, drawn-out moan. Her pulse woke up and started racing.

"Elliot?" she whispered.

"Hmm?" His hushed voice was laced with pain.

Kate threw back the covers and turned to face him. He lay on the outside of the bed he was sharing with both girls, who were snuggled in the middle. A night table sat between the two beds and the alarm clock's numbers blazed 3:33. She couldn't see his face but she could hear his breathing, which had gone shallow and slow.

"Are you alright?" Kate squinted into the darkness.

"Yup," he groaned quietly. "Gracie has really pointy knees and really good aim."

Kate brought her hand to her mouth to stifle a giggle. "I'm sorry. That's not funny."

"Nope. Not funny."

Her chest filled with laughter that begged for release. He took down criminals, busted offenders, watched over their small, beautiful town. And he'd finally been taken out by a sleeping angel with tiny knees.

"You done laughing, Aarons?"

She went up on one elbow. "Almost. Get over here. How can two little girls take up so much space?" she asked, scooting over.

His breathing seemed to have stopped, so she spoke again. "Elliot?"

"What?"

"Come share this bed. The girls are hogging yours."

She held her breath. The waiting gave her time to realize the implications of her offer. Her cheeks warmed right before heat washed over the rest of her body as well. They were friends. It meant nothing. Just a courtesy. But now she couldn't stop thinking about lying beside him, in bed, in the dark.

"I just meant there's no reason we can't share over here. I stay pretty still in my sleep. My knees won't hurt you," she said, making light of it.

A deep sigh was his first response. "I think I better stay right here, Aarons."

There it was again. Like she was a pal on his damn football team. He wouldn't hesitate to share a bed with a buddy, and clearly that's how he wanted her to *think* he saw her. This pricked at her pride like a pin against a balloon. "You sure you know my name?"

His voice was low. "I know your name."

More silence followed, only this one felt charged. She wanted to stretch her fingers out and see if she could reach his bed. Him.

"I won't bite," she said. Unfortunately, she pictured biting him—

just a gentle bite—right under his jaw. It would be slightly scratchy, soft, and she'd feel his pulse beneath her lips.

As the silence stretched on, she second-guessed her offer. Why was she pushing him? Maybe because night time left her lonelier than any other time. She might be happy that she'd broken things off with Darby, the lying-cheating-jackass head of accounting at her fashion house. But the couple of nights he'd managed to stay over (usually he said he had early meetings, and she'd been too caught up in everything to realize he wouldn't, or shouldn't, given his job), Kate had luxuriated in the feel of someone next to her.

She hadn't known she'd enjoy the weight of someone she loved lying beside her. She'd loved sleeping in either of her sisters' beds when she was little, but this had been different. Waking in the darkness next to someone she cared about, being able to curl into them and remind yourself you weren't alone—she missed that far more than anything else about Darby, and she hadn't even known she wanted it. Someone beside her every night, for good. The sound of their breathing lulling her to sleep.

"Kate?"

Her name on his lips brought her back, made her shiver. "Hmm?"

"How come you aren't sleeping?"

Because the sound of you breathing and the hint of your cologne is distracting. "Sometimes I just can't."

"Yeah?"

"Yeah."

"You get screwed over by a guy in New York?"

Her heart screeched to a halt. Damnit. Cops were too nosey and too perceptive. At least, the ones she knew were. "What?"

She heard him rustle and shift, and then she felt the weight of him on her blankets, essentially pinning her under the covers. Now that he was beside her, she couldn't breathe. Well, she could but all of her air was filled with Elliot.

Light from parking lot filtered through the gap in the curtains, and Elliot's eyes flashed like stars in the darkness—sharp, sparkling, intense. She fought the urge to move closer.

"Talk to me."

She'd planned to keep it bottled up. It was history—and no longer part of *her* story. She didn't want a man, a married one at that, to be a focal point of her life and she sure as hell didn't want him to be a reason she'd come unhinged and craved home. She didn't want to feel the shame of being foolish enough not to have known Darby was lying to her the whole time. But it curled in her belly, eating away at her.

Maybe if she told Elliot, she could maintain a hint of composure when she unloaded on her sisters, both of whom had the type of men who were only supposed to exist in romance novels. Hot, sweet, excellent fathers. *Like Elliot.* Her stomach clenched right along with her heart, dueling sensations working against each other.

"Kate?"

"Nothing to tell, really. His name was Darby. He was sweet and funny. After a few dates, we became a couple, or at least I thought we had. I fell for him, but even before I did, I was unsure about staying in New York. I loved the work and still do, but when I was there, even when I was alone, my head felt crowded. There's always so much going on in the city. I'd walk to work or take the subway and feel lost, insignificant. I realized I loved learning about design, and the first time Kael complimented one of my ideas in a meeting, it was awesome." She took a breath as she remembered the feeling of pride, the ownership. It had been a slinky, sky-blue halter dress that shimmered in the right light. "Anyway, I thought, if it's just the work I love, I don't have to be *in* New York to do it. Darby thought my idea for a shop in Angel's Lake was great. He encouraged me, loved my designs—not that he knows fashion. I mean, he's an accountant. But he saw designs every day just by working at a fashion house, and he made me feel like mine stood out."

"They do. I've seen your sketches. I can only imagine the real thing," Elliot whispered.

Focused on the feel of his breath on her face, she scooted closer without intending to.

"Maybe. Anyway, things were heating up and were, I thought, good. And he was so supportive of all my ideas. I took a chance and asked him if he'd ever thought of moving away from the city."

Kate played with the seam of the blanket, her fingers rubbing up and down, trying to figure out what Elliot was thinking just from the way his breathing changed.

"And?"

She shifted, making their arms brush against each other. Tickles traced their way over her skin, leaving her restless. "And he started backing off. He wouldn't return my calls. So I went down to accounting on the bottom floor of our building and asked to see him, which I'd never done—we used to meet in the company cafeteria. The receptionist said he and his wife had a standing Tuesday lunch date and he was expected back soon."

"Fuck," he whispered.

She heard movement before she felt his hand find hers in the dark. He linked their fingers and it felt like a cool cloth on a fresh burn. Painful, but soothing a deeper hurt.

"The receptionist asked if I wanted to leave a message."

"Oh no," Elliot whispered, humor tinting the words—most of the town knew the Aarons sisters weren't real great at hiding their feelings.

"What?" She whispered back, smiling into the darkness and enjoying the feel and the shape of his fingers.

"What'd you do?"

"Nothing," she said, her pitch a bit higher. "Just left a message for him saying I hoped he had a really great lunch with his wife."

"Shit."

Kate laughed. "He emailed about forty times after that, the idiot. We'd dated for a few months and he'd thought he was in the clear, mostly because I was too stupid to pay attention. Then when I found out and left a message that I know, he panicked. I have enough emails to throw his marriage down the tubes. But that's not my place. And it's not what I wanted."

"You ever email him back?"

"Nope. He came up to see me. I told Kael I didn't want to talk to him. No one gets around Kael to one of his girls—and seeing as he thinks of Lucy as one of his own sisters, he considers me one of those girls."

"Sorry, Kate." His fingers tightened on hers and this time he was the one who closed the space.

He was fully in her breathing space now and Kate imagined being closer, burrowing into him and feeling the heat of his skin against her own, the touch of his lips somewhere other than her forehead. Her other hand lifted in slow motion, reaching out for him. One of the girls snored, a tiny, snuffling sound, and both Elliot and Kate froze. When she quieted, both of them released heavy breaths.

Focusing on his fingers touching hers, she kept going, telling him what she didn't want to say out loud to anyone. "It's not that it didn't work out or I got my heart broken. It's that I didn't *see*. That I was naïve enough to think, hey, this great, good-looking guy, this New-York-City-successful guy, wants *me*. And now I can't stop questioning my own judgement. My own ability to see what's right in front of me. I hate it. I hate knowing I…stained their marriage that way." Kate blinked away the tears. "Cliché right?"

Elliot's tone stiffened along with his body. "He's a dickhead. Hard to learn the truth about someone when they keep it hidden. You see the good in people. That's the part you focus on. Not like you won't accept flaws, but when someone is underhanded enough to conceal them, you're not the type to dig, wondering if they're there. And New York City doesn't make someone special. Who they are and how they treat people does. You're special, Kate. And any guy that doesn't get that is a fucking idiot."

His words took away some of the sting. "Still. Cliché and stupid on my part."

"Nothing stupid or cliché about you, Kate. Real men—good men— don't cheat, insecure ones do. He's an ass and that's on him. Says nothing about you."

"It says I didn't look close enough. I was so happy having a grown-up life: living in New York, working in fashion, carrying on a relationship. But none of it was real. I mean, it was, but the parts that were didn't feel like it and the parts that weren't, did."

"Uh…you want to say that one more time for me, sweetheart? It's almost four in the morning and I can't decipher girl logic."

Kate pulled her hand from his so she could smack him on the shoulder, but also so she could focus on something other than the way his term of endearment felt like being folded into his arms and held tight. His silent laughter shook the bed.

"The fashion part of it was surreal. Models walking around in their underwear, half their make-up on, waiting to try on the next outfit, complaining about the cold, stripping down in front of each other. I would be taking measurements and making adjustments one second and the next, I was holding their phones so they could squeeze into a design or slip on five-inch heels. I mean, most of them are so tall anyway, the heels seem like overkill. But they really do make the outfits. It was crazy, like being on the set of a reality show."

Elliot made a humming noise. "That sounds like a terrible way to spend a day. How'd you get that internship again?"

He'd taken her hand again and this time, when she tried to pull it free, he held strong.

"I'm teasing. Really. I would hate to spend my time around half-naked models. Go on."

"You're real funny, aren't you?"

"Only in the middle of the night."

All too aware of the way his laughter and the pressure of his fingers were distracting her, she tried to explain herself. "It was everything I imagined. It was amazing and at first, I loved the crazy pace. I learned so much about designing and materials and the industry in general. It didn't feel real. It was like I'd been plopped down into the dream I'd created in my head. And I feel like I didn't fully wake up enough to enjoy it before I realized it wasn't for me. I mean, fashion is, but not there. Not in New York and not like that."

Keeping her hand in his, Elliot shifted so he was on his back, and now that her eyes had adjusted to the dark, Kate watched as he put his other hand behind his head, still listening.

"Darby was really just a footnote. We laughed and had fun. It was good. I was living the exact life I thought I wanted, but every night when I got home to my studio, which I could barely afford, I wished I could pop over to my mom and dad's and snag dinner or babysit my nieces. I'm worried I didn't try hard enough. That I wasted the opportunity I was given and if I did, maybe I didn't even deserve to have that chance. I'm scared I'm going home to disappoint my family. Which I already did when I left for New York. So it's like full circle but not in a good way."

She listened to his breathing and it calmed some of the turbulence in her chest. It was good to confide in someone who didn't mind listening and wouldn't feel sorry for her or irritated with her choices. Lucy had gotten her the contact. What if Kael was mad at Lucy for recommending her little sister? What if Darby said something about her and Kate's name was already spinning on the wheel of gossip? What if she was seen as flighty, and the bank in Angel's Lake wouldn't give her a loan without her parents' signatures for back up?

"I think anything that solidifies who you are and who you want to be can't be a waste."

"Do you really think that? I mean I'm turning twenty-five and I don't even have a job."

Elliot gave a low, rough chuckle. "Twenty-five is definitely heading over the hill. But I think you're good. You've got a degree, a plan, and a family who'll back you no matter what." He squeezed her hand. "And you have friends who'll do the same."

She nodded, thinking about his words. She hadn't been sleeping well for a while now, but most of the nights she'd lain awake, her heart felt like it was tap dancing in her chest. Right now, she felt content. Unburdened. She was going home. Somehow, things would be okay.

"How about you? You think all of the things that led you to where you are right now were worth it?"

Elliot let go of her hand and crossed his arms over his chest. Kate scrunched her pillow a bit under her neck, hoping he'd answer.

"Gina's a mess. I need to get my girls settled into a real life. They're in first grade now. They need to be at school, the same school, every day. They need to come home, do homework, have dinner, and go to bed at the same time each night. They need routine."

"They need you."

He turned his head. She was already looking at him but now their eyes found each other.

"They do. I was unsure of that before. I mean, I work odd hours and overtime. I thought we could do this together even if we weren't a couple. I try to be a good parent; I would do anything for them. And I thought letting them be with their mom without boundaries was what I was supposed to do, but I was wrong. She hasn't changed. Gina has always been one hundred percent about herself. I don't even think she realizes it. That's the worst part. She's always surprised when her choices backfire and hurt others. But even knowing that, I can't regret it because of them."

She hated how his voice dipped low, more pained than angry, and she wondered if he ever missed the woman he'd fallen for—not the mother of his girls, but the woman she'd been before.

"Why didn't you ever marry her?"

Kate wondered if she'd gone too far, but Elliot reached out and touched her hip in reassurance, heating the spot with just the touch of his fingers. Just as quickly, he pulled his hand back.

"I was never sure about the wife and two-point-five kids deal. At the time, we were just hooking up, having fun. When Gina told me she was pregnant, I was all in. The problem was, she wasn't. Still, I was willing to try hard enough for the both of us. But a relationship can't work like that and neither can parenting. She moved in with me and that…well, it was a disaster. At first, I put it down to pregnancy—her irritability, unhappiness, her need to pick up and go, the way she changed her mind every five seconds and never seemed satisfied with anything. As much as I loved Grace and Beth from the second they were born, I couldn't marry Gina. I couldn't promise myself to her if I could so easily imagine my life without her in it. The first time she took off, the girls were six months old. When she came back after two weeks, there was nothing romantic between us. She didn't love me. Ever, I think."

Kate bit her lip and then took the jump. "Did you ever love her?"

Even in the dark, she could see his eyes were sad. "I don't think so. Not the way I should love a woman I have two children with. I'm sad for her. She's missing out on the only good things that ever came from us meeting. I've tried to fill in the gaps, make excuses for her not showing up when she says she will or forgetting promises she's made the girls. But I'm done. She had her chance and now it's my turn. I'm going for custody, and I think I'll get it, mostly because I don't even think she wants it."

Kate thought she'd been a fool, but Gina definitely took the gold there. "They're so lucky to have you, Elliot."

When he smiled, Kate curled her fingers into her arm so she wouldn't reach out to him.

"We need to get through Christmas and then figure out daycare, afterschool care, that sort of thing. It won't be easy. But it'll be right."

Kate rolled onto her back and burrowed a little deeper into the covers.

"I've looked into it before," Elliot said. "It's expensive to put kids in daycare, but with them in school all day, maybe it won't be so bad.

It would basically be after-school care and maybe some holidays. Plus, your family actually said they could help out a bit with picking up from school and stuff. You come from a good place, Aarons."

She shook her head against the pillow. Back to Aarons. When she was Kate, he could hold her hand and steal her breath. But when she was Aarons, they were locked in the no-touch friend zone. When things started to get more intimate, it was like he had to remind himself to switch between gears.

"I do. They're good people and they mean it when they say they'll help. I can too, you know."

"Yeah? How are you with decorating? I need to get a tree up pronto."

Kate jackknifed into a sitting position, mouth open, and looked down at him. "You don't have a tree up? What is wrong with you?"

"I've been a little busy. And I didn't know for sure they were going to be with me over the holidays."

Kate got out of bed and padded to the fridge. She grabbed two bottles of water and brought them back, crawling on top of the covers. "You should be ashamed of yourself. It's just over two weeks until Christmas. Fifteen days, Elliot."

"I'm sorry?"

"Tell me you've shopped."

"Uh. Mostly?"

She sank back on the bed and sighed. "You are so lucky I'm coming home. Christmas is magic and miracles and you need decorations. Everywhere. Don't you want your girls to experience all the wonder of Christmas?"

He sat up, leaned against the headboard and took one of the waters she passed him.

"There's still time, Kate."

She scoffed, quietly. "Clearly, you're a guy."

"Um. I thought that was clear before this conversation."

The amusement in his voice didn't escape her. Neither did his guyness. Kate had tagged along the day Lucy had done a calendar photo shoot with a bunch of the men from the community to raise money to rebuild the town rec center, which had burned down. It had definitely brought in the funds. Elliot had been there, shirtless, along with Lucy's now-husband, Char's husband, and a few others. And Kate's memory of Elliot was forever tattooed on her brain. Even now, she could easily picture his defined abs, the smooth ridges dusted with dark hair leading into the waistband of basketball shorts that clung to his hips.

"Kate?"

She blinked and cleared her throat. "What?"

"You were complaining about me being male at Christmas. I'm admitting my folly and asking if you'd mind shopping with me for the girls. You love shopping—which is a flaw I'll overlook because I want to use it to my advantage. Plus, you shop for your nieces all the time. I didn't exactly grow up with all of the Christmas trimmings, but I know your mom doesn't do anything halfway."

"No, she really doesn't. And Christmas is the absolute best. Of course I'll help you. You definitely need all the help you can get." Taking a sip of her water, she ignored the way his laugh did funny things to her stomach—like he was running his hand along her skin, chasing goose bumps. She shivered again.

"Cold?"

Not even a little bit. "Nope. But I'm tired."

He nodded and crawled out of the bed. Kate frowned.

"You can sleep with me," she said. As soon as she said the words aloud, she squeezed her eyes shut, wishing she could take them back.

"I mean, beside me. In the same bed." Elliot stared at her, his mouth dropping open slightly. As she continued to babble and gesture to his daughters, one dark eyebrow raised. "I mean so your...your junk is safe. So you don't get kicked. I won't kick you. Oh, my God. Make me stop talking. Tell me to shut up. Make it stop."

Elliot stood, laughing and shaking his head. Kate held herself very still, hoping that maybe she'd disappear into the weird flower pattern of the comforter. Just when she thought she might be able to breathe again, Elliot leaned over, hooked his fingers around her neck, and tilted her head back. Her breath caught in her throat and her eyes closed as his lips, Elliot's soft, warm lips, touched her forehead.

"I think it's safer with the girls."

Kate nodded as he pulled away. The spot he'd kissed tingled with warmth, and Kate got under the covers, trying to pretend she hadn't spoken. Her stomach tightened. Grabbing a pillow, she tossed it at him as he settled into bed.

"What's this for?"

"Protection."

Elliot laughed and though she couldn't see him as well now, she bet that even his eyes were laughing, which was far better than being offended by her implication

"Thanks for keeping my junk safe, Aarons."

"It's the least I could do." *Or I could just stop talking and claim insanity in the morning.*

"Good night, Kate. I'm glad you joined us for the ride."

Her stomach stopped seizing, and a tranquil kind of pleasure washed over her. "Thanks. Me too. Good night."

She fell asleep trying very hard not to think about Elliot, his body parts, or the feeling of his lips against her skin.

Chapter Five

Kate opened one eye to the feeling of a little finger tapping her on the shoulder. Grace leaned over the side of the bed, into her and whispered loudly, "Are you awake?"

Kate closed her eye and buried her cheek into the pillow. "Not really. You okay?"

Grace curled into her side, shifting, turning, and burrowing into Kate like she belonged right in the spot between her body and her arm. Grace's head shared Kate's pillow and her little hand was on top of where Kate's now rested on Grace's belly.

Opening her eyes, it was easy to smile down at Elliot's older-by-two-minutes daughter. "You comfy, sweetheart?"

Grace nodded. "Santa is coming soon."

"That's right. And tonight we'll be home," Kate whispered back. Glancing over, she saw Elliot still asleep with Beth burrowed into his body, much like Grace was with Kate. A pang of…*God, what was that?* Need or want or *something* shot through her hard, like a jolt of electricity.

"We didn't get Daddy a present yet. Can you help us? Me and Beth have ten dollars. Aunt Shelly paid us five each to go watch TV."

Kate closed her eyes and counted to ten. Grace shifted, so she was on her back, looking up at Kate. When she opened her eyes and looked back into Gracie's, she hoped her irritation didn't show. "Of course I'll help you. We'll figure it out when we get home, okay?"

Grace nodded again. "I'm hungry."

Just like that, the topic switched, and Kate wished she could turn her thoughts on a dime that way. Instead, she yawned and stretched. "There's a restaurant. We can go get pancakes."

Grace sat up, nodding her head frantically. "I love pancakes. I'll wake Beth and Daddy."

Kate glanced over again and took in the sight of Elliot sprawled on the bed, his eyelashes fanning out over his cheeks in his sleep. He wore a dark green T-shirt and one of his hands was dangling off the bed. Beth was beginning to stir.

"Why don't you just wake Beth? Let your daddy sleep. We still have a long ride."

Grace tiptoed over to Beth while Kate pulled herself from the bed, grabbed her carry-on, and went to the washroom. She brushed her teeth, tied her long, dark hair up into a ponytail, and washed her face. Sliding into a bra, she figured there was no harm in all three of them heading to the restaurant in pajamas. She finished up and opened the door, still moving quietly.

She nearly squealed when her eyes met Elliot's wide-awake ones. His quiet laugh sent a delicious shiver over her skin.

"Hey." His dark eyes were drowsy as they watched her. Leaning on his elbow and hip, his blanket trailed down and his shirt had bunched, treating Kate to a view of the abs she remembered very well. Her eyes followed the ridges before she remembered herself and snapped her gaze back up to his.

Kate kept her eyes firmly on his face. "Hey. We were going to grab some breakfast. Why don't you go back to sleep?"

"Daddy doesn't like mornings unless he's going to the beach," Grace said, putting her shoes on.

He might not enjoy early hours, but he looked damn good in the morning. "I don't really blame him," Kate answered.

"I can get up," Elliot said, starting to do just that.

She held up a hand. "Sleep." It was the least she could do for hijacking his trip. It would also put some distance between her and his abs.

Beth walked over and thrust a shoe up so Kate could see it. "I can't get this undone," she said.

"Then ask for help politely, Beth," Elliot said.

Kate untangled the knot and handed the shoe to Beth, who murmured, "thank you."

"You sure?" Elliot's eyes searched Kate's.

Pretending the weight of his stare didn't unlock guarded places inside of her, she made a dismissive gesture. "I got this. You're driving so you can use the extra rest."

"Thanks."

The girls gave him noisy kisses and Kate wondered if he'd be able to fall back asleep. She never could. Once she was up, she was up. Beth and Grace chattered all the way down the horribly patterned hallway.

"We haven't seen Santa yet," Beth said as Kate pressed the button for the elevator.

Kate gestured for both girls to go in before her. "I'm sure there's time. Did you write letters?"

"I'm pressing the button," Grace shouted.

"It's my turn," Beth said.

"No, it's mine," Grace answered.

Kate put a hand on each of their shoulders. "Shh. People are still sleeping. Grace, press the button. Beth, you press it on the way back up."

Beth gave a small "hmph," while Grace pressed the rounded two. Kate smiled down at them, thinking it would be lovely to have such minor worries.

"We didn't write letters," Grace said.

"Well, there's still time for all of that," Kate said, wondering if she should mention it to Elliot.

"No there isn't," Beth said, still frowning.

"Why don't we write them while we wait for breakfast?" Kate asked.

Both girls beamed, their smiles overtaking their entire faces, twin smiles that caused happiness to simmer in her. *Adorable.*

They settled down with menus, and Kate ordered a vat of coffee. Once they'd placed their orders, pancakes for both girls and waffles for Kate, they got down to the serious business of penning letters to Santa on the back of their kid's menus.

"Are you writing one, Kate?" Beth asked.

Grace had her pen resting on her lips, her eyes scrunched in thought. "She can't write one. She's a grown-up."

Kate nodded. "Santa brings stuff to kids. Grown-ups take care of each other," Kate said.

Beth looked at her sister. "But we can still ask for stuff for Daddy, right?"

Grace looked at Kate, who opened her mouth then closed it. Maybe she should have waited on this. Every family had different traditions, though she wondered if Elliot and the girls did. Kate knew he had a rocky relationship with his own parents and wasn't close to them. He didn't have the girls every Christmas either, Gina and he had shared.

Kate went with her gut and hoped she wasn't overstepping. "I'm sure you can ask for something for him but Santa can't guarantee anything. Why don't you just write your letter and I bet he'll do the best he can." *There. Open ended.*

"If you're asking for something for Daddy, so am I. What are you going to ask for?" Beth said.

"I want Santa to bring him a puppy," Grace said.

Kate laughed, nearly choking on her coffee. "Wow. That would be fun for him, wouldn't it?" She didn't think Elliot wanted a gift that spread his attentions any thinner.

"If he got a puppy, we could take care of it for him," Beth said.

Grace nodded excitedly. "I'm going to ask for a puppy for me, too."

Beth rolled her eyes comically. "You can't ask for two puppies."

Grace frowned. "It's not two. One would stay with Daddy all the time and the other one comes with us when we go to Mommy's."

Kate listened to their banter, letting the caffeine work its magic.

"We're not going back and forth anymore. Daddy told Mommy he was done with that and if she wanted to see us she'd have to come to Angel's Lake," Grace told her sister.

Kate's eyebrows rose. She wondered if Elliot had meant for the girls to hear that.

"Mommy doesn't like it there," Beth said.

Grace shrugged. Her eyes shimmered with sadness and she looked down at the pen she was holding, twisting it in her grip. "That's just too bad. Because that's where we'll be."

Beth said nothing to that, and Kate's heart squeezed. Trying to lighten the mood, she wrote something down on her own list.

"Oh, I have a good one," she said, covering her words with her hand.

Both Beth and Grace were immediately distracted from their gloom.

"What is it?"

"Do you want a puppy too?"

Kate laughed and glanced at both of them. "Actually, I would love a puppy, but my wish is that you both have the very merriest, bestest Christmas ever."

Both of the girls giggled as two servers brought their meals.

"Bestest isn't a word, Kate, but I'm going to ask Santa to bring you a puppy too," Grace said, her smile wide and toothy.

"All right, pancakes for you two ladies and waffles for Mom," one of the servers said.

"Oh," Kate said before surprise stopped her words.

"She's not our mom. She's our Kate," Beth said.

A rush of warmth filled Kate's chest, making her feel like she might burst.

"Well, you're both so cute, that sounds like a good thing to be as well," the waitress said. Kate saw the apology in her eyes when their gazes met.

Grace dug into her pancakes, more ripping them apart with her fork and knife than cutting them, while Beth asked for help. Kate was just pushing Beth's plate back to her when she saw Elliot out of the corner of her eye.

She took a moment to drink him in at a distance. There had to be something in the water in Angel's Lake because it was home to some seriously fine-looking men, but none of the others had ever made her pulse sprint quite like Elliot Peters did. His dark hair was tousled, like his fingers had traveled through it a few times. A bit of scruff outlined his strong jaw and those smoky, dark eyes were pinning Kate to her seat. *Jesus. Breathe.* The sight of him strolling over in a pair of cargo pants and a cozy gray hoodie was almost better than caffeine. She picked up her cup, gulped some down. *Almost.*

"Mind if I join you girls?" Elliot's eyes stayed on Kate even as he spoke to his daughters.

Grace and Beth looked up, mouths full, and said, "Daddy!" at the same time. Elliot laughed, leaned over to kiss them both on the head, and then gestured to Kate to move over.

All thought fled her brain for a second before she realized she'd frozen. She laughed too loudly and scooted over on the booth's padded seat. He slid in and his thigh brushed up against her pajama-clad one. *It's just the fleece that's making you warm. If you can share a bed, you can share a padded seat. Actually, don't think about sharing a bed.*

Without asking, Elliot took her coffee and swallowed down the rest of it. She eyed him as he set the mug down, clearing her lust-filled vision.

"You always wake up with a death wish?"

He tugged a lock of her hair and grinned. Her stomach bounced at the sight of that smile—it went all the way up to his eyes.

"I'll buy you another," he said, winking.

The waitress came by and asked if he'd like a coffee and some food. Without even looking at the menu, he ordered eggs, bacon, toast, pancakes, and coffee. Kate grinned as their server walked away.

"Wow. Sleeping sure gives you an appetite," she said.

Elliot's eyes locked on hers. Kate's breath caught. One beat. Two.

Then she remembered to breathe.

"Daddy, we're writing letters to Santa," Grace said.

"Hey, that's a pretty good idea. We can mail them when we get back to Angel's Lake. What'd you ask him for? Wait. Have you been good?"

The girls giggled. "I have," Beth said.

"Hey! I have too," Grace said.

Elliot smiled then looked at Kate again. "How about you, Kate?"

Feelings tumbled in her chest and clogged her throat. *Nope, not really. I've messed up a fair amount and really want to mess up worse. With you.* "Of course," she said.

Elliot's food arrived quickly and he dug in. The girls asked to go to the bathroom, insisting they couldn't wait until they were back in the room and that they had to go together. Since the bathrooms were directly across the restaurant in his eyesight, Elliot told them they could go on their own. He'd probably be protective even if he weren't a cop or a dad. Some things were just part of a person's make-up.

"They're just so sweet," Kate said, watching the girls link hands.

"They really are." Elliot looked down at his food, pushing some hash browns around on the plate.

"You okay?"

"I've gotten used to Gina making me scramble, but I can usually hide it from the girls. She was supposed to keep them through Christmas. She begged me to let her have the holiday. So I agreed to work Christmas Day to keep my mind off missing them. Next thing I know, she's quit another job and taken them across state lines. Then she calls me because her sister doesn't want them there. My girls shouldn't be at the mercy of whatever whim she dreams up. I just want to make Christmas great for them."

Kate hated the jaded tone of his voice. It didn't suit his temperament.

Covering his hand with her own, she squeezed.

"They *will* have a great Christmas. You're a fantastic dad, and you'll deal with the rest after the holidays. One step at a time. And you're not alone. Being currently unemployed, I have ample time on my hands to help you out."

Elliot turned his hand so their fingers linked. "Thanks, Kate. I was happy for you when you got to go to New York, but I'm glad you're coming home. It's not the same there without you. And I actually have some ideas for how you could help me out."

Wondering what he meant by that, Kate nodded, biting her lip to block the unexpected rush of emotion clogging her throat. The girls returned before she could say anything else. Once Elliot finished eating and Kate downed a third cup of coffee, he paid for the meal—ignoring Kate's protests—and they returned to the room to grab their things. They loaded up Elliot's truck and got the girls settled before Kate grabbed his iPhone to make a playlist.

Traveling with the girls required turning around frequently to answer questions, pass them something, or open snacks for them. After about the fifth time, Kate's stomach rolled uncomfortably.

She rested her head back against the seat, closed her eyes and sighed heavily. When Elliot's hand touched her thigh, her eyes popped open.

"You okay?"

He put his hand back on the steering wheel and she found her voice. "Hmm. Just too much turning around, I think."

He gave her a quick frown before returning his attention to the road. Kate must have nodded off with the girls because when she opened her eyes again, they were just outside Angel's Lake. Checking the back, she saw the girls were out.

"Sleeping Beauty awakes," Elliot said quietly.

Kate yawned, covering her mouth. "Sorry about that. Not the best wingman, am I, Maverick?"

He laughed. "Um…are you still asleep?"

Shaking her head, she stared at him. "What?"

He switched on his signal and took a right onto the main road into Angel's Lake. "What are you talking about?"

Firming her lips, she tried to clear her sleep-fogged brain. "Maverick? Goose?"

Elliot's laughed. "Aarons, did you hit your head on the window?"

"You should be ashamed."

Shaking his head, his eyes crinkled at the corners and his lips turned up in a small smirk. "And maybe you ought to go back to sleep."

"*Top Gun*. Tell me you've seen it."

He smacked the steering wheel. "Right. Yes. Saw it. Don't remember that part."

She groaned. "Stop talking."

Elliot laughed. "Don't give up on me. Hey, if you're the wingman, does that make me Tom Cruise?"

"Yes. But if you jump on a couch, I'm spreading it through town that you don't know your *Top Gun* trivia."

His laughter fueled hers. He nodded. "Noted." Then he poked her in the shoulder and added, "I'm terribly sorry I've disappointed you in my knowledge of movies. I'll make it up to you."

That sounded far too tempting. Kate considered. "I'll accept your apology but you'll need to watch the movie with me to really make up for it."

"Sounds fair."

Kate laughed and watched the familiar sights come into view. An ache settled just under her chest. She'd been home last Christmas and thought her homesickness was just from the long stretch of time she'd been away. Missing her family was normal; they were close. Even when her sister Lucy had traveled, they'd stayed in touch.

But New York had kept her so busy. She'd tried to absorb everything she could about fashion and design and the industry in general. In the moments she had to herself, she'd made it to some of the more touristy sights, but usually, a day to herself meant running errands and catching up on sleep. But in the back of her mind, in the corner of her heart, she'd never felt truly at home in the city. Because there was only one of those and this was it. Sure, she wanted things Angel's Lake didn't offer right now. But if her plans worked out, she'd have everything she ever dreamed of, right in the small town where she'd grown up.

"You know, if you'd referenced *Fast and Furious*, I'd have impressed you." Elliot pulled up to her parents' house and put the car in park.

"What?" The pressure in her chest increased and Kate rubbed the heel of her hand between her breasts.

"Paul Walker? Vin Diesel?"

Elliot's easy humor diverted the ache in her chest and made her laugh again. He was good at that. "You're making it worse. Stop it."

He undid his seatbelt and turned toward her, taking her hand from where she was pressing it. His hand dwarfed hers and she felt the calluses brush over her soft skin.

"Joking. You okay?"

She nodded and bit her lip. She would be. Right after she told her whole family she was home to stay and some days she wished she'd never left. It looked like she'd get that over in one shot, as Luke and Char's cars were parked on the road.

"Nervous. Stupid right?"

His hand on hers was reassuring. He squeezed and her eyes moved up to his. "Not stupid. Normal. Everything happens for a reason, right?" He glanced out the window and frowned.

"You think?"

Elliot looked down at their hands and Kate's stomach danced. "I do. I have to remind myself of that repeatedly. I can remind you when you forget."

"I might take you up on that."

"Daddy, where are we?"

Kate and Elliot turned to see Beth was waking up, rubbing her eyes.

"We're home, sweet pea. Well, we're at Kate's home. But we'll be at ours in ten minutes."

"You gotta go, Kate?"

"I do. But I'll see you guys…" she started then turned to Elliot. "When do you want to do the tree and decorations?"

"Tomorrow work? I want to talk to you about something anyway."

Kate scrunched her nose up, pursing her lips as she stared at him. *Why is he being so cryptic*? She couldn't think about it right now with the girls waking up and her nerves battering her insides.

Kate gave both girls a smile. "I'll see you both tomorrow. We'll put up a tree and I'll tell you about all of the fun things my family does at Christmas. Then we'll make your daddy do them, okay?"

"Okay," Beth said, her toothy smile widening.

Elliot shook his head, getting out of the truck.

"See you girls tomorrow," Kate said.

They spoke in unison. "Bye, Kate."

Elliot had her bag out of the back by the time she came around the truck. She'd forgotten what noiseless city streets were like.

"Thank you for driving me."

He passed the bag. "My pleasure. Thanks for the company. You sure about tomorrow?"

Her gaze had caught on the fullness of his lips. When she glanced up, she saw he was watching her with an amused expression.

"Kate?"

"Yeah?"

"Tomorrow?"

She nodded. "Yes. Tree. Christmas. *Top Gun* and mystery conversation."

His laugh cut through the quiet as he pulled her into a one-armed hug. "Sounds perfect. Say hi to everyone for me."

She watched his truck pull away from the curb and then she turned and stared at the house where she'd grown up. Kate had been so scared to leave and take off on a grand adventure. She'd earned a degree in social work and then said goodbye to her hometown and her family to follow a dream she'd kept hidden from everyone.

And now she was home. Nerves pulsated like a heartbeat, making her feel weighted and empty at the same time.

"How long are you going to stand there?"

Kate turned, her heart singing at the sound of her sister's voice. Lucy stood, covered in a ridiculous parka, the hood pulled up around her gorgeous face. Lucy's smile could light up all of Angel's Lake and seeing it, knowing she was home, flipped a switch inside of Kate. She burst into tears.

Chapter Six

Kate squeezed her sister so hard she was probably cutting off Lucy's air. She didn't seem to mind though, and returned Kate's embrace with just as much strength.

She couldn't stop the tears that fell onto Lucy's sweater.

Lucy leaned back, keeping her hands on Kate's shoulders. "You okay?"

Nodding was the best Kate could do. Lucy tugged her close again. "You look good. New York City good. I'm so glad you're home."

Tell her now. Then you can start working on getting her to forgive you. Against Lucy's shoulder, Kate mumbled her words.

"I'm not going back."

Lucy released her, but stayed close. "Okay." Her eyebrows drew down, like she was confused, or waiting for more.

She'd missed Lucy's face. She'd missed all of them. Kate chatted with them on FaceTime and Skype. She talked to her mom or one of her sisters every few days. But it wasn't the same as being in front of them. *With* them. God, was she ever going to grow up and stop needing her family?

"Kate?"

The words rushed out, eager to escape. "I can't go back, Luce. It was awesome and wonderful, but I want to be home. Even at my happiest there, I felt lonely. Like something was missing. Whatever I do with fashion and design, I need to do it here where you guys are. I need to be *home*. I'm sorry. I'm so sorry."

Lucy nodded. She didn't look mad and that sent a spark of hope into Kate's heart. Lucy spoke before she could. "You obviously need to get this off your chest before we go in, but I'm freezing here, so hurry up and tell me the part that is supposed to surprise or shock me. And why are you sorry?"

Kate stared at her sister. *Could it be this easy?* "You got me the internship and connected me with Kael. I never would have had that without you. He was doing you a favor and then I just up and leave. I let both of you down." There. She'd said it. The pain of the words still sliced through her chest. She was the responsible one, the focused go-getter. Yet in the last two years, she'd wasted her parents' hard-earned money on a social work degree, only to take off to New York because she dreamed of being the next Kate Spade. When she realized she'd only ever be Kate Aarons, small town girl personified, it had been a harrowing blow. But Lucy didn't seem troubled by it at all.

In fact, she laughed. The sound floated through the air like the snowflakes falling. Lucy hugged her again fiercely, and it soothed some of the ache in Kate's chest.

"Welcome home, honey. Who am I to question where you think you need to be?"

A lump lodged in Kate's throat. She swallowed around it but it wouldn't budge. "You're not mad?"

She felt Lucy shake her head. "No. And you hardly fled the city. You finished everything you were working on. Kael was sorry to see you go but he isn't upset. I'm happy you're home. It took me ten years to realize it was the only place to be for the rest of my life. Sometimes you need to go away to find out where you should end up. I'm glad it didn't take you as long."

Kate gripped her sister's sweater, inhaling the scent of cinnamon and cold air. "I always was quicker than you."

Lucy pulled back and put her arm through Kate's, tugging her toward their parents' back porch steps. "Maybe. But now that you're home, Mom can try out her latest tricks and tips on you."

Kate groaned. "I won't be staying here long. It feels like…falling backwards. If I have to stay in my old room more than a few nights, I'll regress."

Lucy nudged her with her shoulder. "I understand, trust me. But about your room, have you talked to Mom and Dad?"

Kate was thinking about how Lucy had done her own soul-searching-find-your-dream whirlwind. And it had landed her right back in Angel's Lake. *So, maybe I'm not so far from where I'm meant to be.* Lucy was staring at her and Kate realized she'd asked a question.

"No, why?"

"Uh, you haven't heard about Char and Luke's house?"

"No. What's wrong?"

Lucy put her arm through Kate's. "I'll tell you later. Let's just focus on you being home and go inside."

Like a camera zooming in, everything was pushed to the background when she and Lucy stepped into the noise and chaos of a family brunch. Motion stopped, reminding Kate of the game she played in high school drama class—Freeze Frame. Like a comedic tableau, her family stared at her from their varying spots around the table and kitchen.

Her mother was wiping something off Emma's adorable cheeks. Her father was passing Alex a can of cola. Carmen, Charlotte's older daughter, was looking at a book with Luke. Mia, also two and adorable, was banging blocks on Emma's high chair tray. All eyes were on Kate. Breathing and talking were suspended, making the pounding of Kate's heart sound like fireworks in her ears. And then everyone moved at once.

Julie Aarons reached her first. "You're here! All three of my girls in one place again. Finally."

Something about her mother's hugs made everything inside of Kate regress. She clung to her mom's shoulders and let herself be rocked, coddled, and soothed. Julie didn't know she was settling the turbulence in Kate's heart; that's just the way her mother was. Kate had forgotten how grateful she was for Julie's exuberant style of hugging.

She choked out a laugh. "Mom," she said. "I can't breathe."

"That's your problem, not mine," Julie answered.

Like she was on an assembly line, she was shifted and shuttled right into her dad's arms. Mark Aarons pulled her close. If Julie was the calm for her storm, Mark was the shield that tried to protect her from it. Her dad's hug pushed everything else away.

"There's my baby. God, I didn't even realize how much I missed you."

Kate nodded against his shoulder. Not even a whisper could fit through the lump stuck in her throat.

Charlotte's eyes were already rimmed with tears by her turn. "Did you bring me pretty clothes?"

Kate laughed but before she could respond, Carmen looked up from her book. "Mommy, we're not supposed to ask people for gifts."

Luke chuckled and rubbed Carmen's shoulder. "Auntie Kate is different, honey. Say hi."

Carmen hesitated, then almost smiled before looking back at her book. "Hi."

Luke tugged Char's sleeve and gave Kate a noisy kiss before squeezing her tight.

Finally, Alex stood in front of her, grinning quietly, his eyes watchful. "You good?"

Kate nodded. "I will be after I get hugging you guys out of the way so I can pick up those babies."

He made it quick and Kate plopped herself between Emma and Mia. They'd grown so much since she'd last seen and held them.

Carmen was engrossed in a very colorful book on penguins, probably absorbing every detail and ounce of knowledge the book had to offer.

Kate touched her shoulder gently then turned back to Mia, who grabbed at her hair. Emma, not to be outdone, pointed at Mia and squealed.

"Baby," Emma said. Then kept saying it.

The laughter and happiness in the room pushed all of Kate's worries out of her mind and out of her heart like she'd placed them on a conveyer belt and shipped them to the next stop. She knew they'd catch up with her again, but for now, she was with her family. She was home.

Chapter Seven

Elliot fisted both hands on his hips and dipped his chin to his chest. He counted to ten in his head and listened to his breathing. In. Out. In. Out. They were still fighting. He broke up domestic disputes and goddamn bar fights and his twins were going to get the better of him.

Since the Jedi-mind-trick/Zen strategy was not working, he stepped through the door of their shared room. A bomb of clothing and toys had exploded and eviscerated the floor.

He kept his eyes on them. "Stop!"

Gracie and Beth froze, almost comically, their respective hands still latched onto either side of a small, cloth rag doll with reggae hair, a stitched-on face, and a blue dress.

Grace looked like she wanted to rip it apart, and Beth's eyes were full of unshed tears. Elliot stomped over a pile of dresses and skirts, sidestepped a hairbrush and thrust out his hand, palm up.

"Give it."

Both girls launched to their feet still holding the damn doll.

"Daddy, I had it first, and it's my turn to sleep with it," Beth said.

Grace gave a useless tug. "You slept with it in the car yesterday."

"That doesn't count," Beth said. Her eyes were pleading with Elliot.

"Give it," he said, his tone even and calm, even though inside he felt like this room looked: an utter disaster. It hadn't even been two nights yet.

The girls sighed in unison and handed it to him. He squeezed it and brought it closer for inspection while they stared at him. It wasn't their best doll, not by a long shot. It had woolen strands for hair, a cloth dress that was ripped, two real buttons, a mini pocket, and what looked like painted-on shoes.

"Where'd we get her?" Elliot asked, holding the doll up to face them.

"Aunt Shelly gave it to us," Grace said. She looked down at the pile of clothes under her feet, then back up.

Elliot tried not to frown on the outside. "One doll for the two of you?"

"Yes," Beth said, her lip trembling. "She said one day we'll probably share boys so we could start practicing with a doll."

"Jesus Christ," Elliot muttered, unfortunately aloud.

Both girls' eyes went wide. *Shit.* He was so tired that even if he didn't have twins, he'd probably see two of them. He was lucky he wasn't seeing four. Alex had given him today off, thankfully, but he hadn't slept much the night before. Every time he'd closed his eyes, he saw Kate's sweet smile. When he did catch a bit of dreamtime, his mind was filled with horrible visions of forgetting to fill the girls' stockings or put their Christmas presents under the tree. The girls continued to stare and it wasn't their fault he was tired. They were too, and he needed to cover his tracks and shift the mood.

"Nothing. It's His birthday," Elliot said.

"Huh?" Beth narrowed her eyes at him. She wasn't buying his story, and he obviously hadn't needed the cover.

Elliot turned, doll in hand, and waved them out of the room. "Come on. We're forgetting the meaning of Christmas. You're in there fighting, giving me and this doll a headache, and we should be getting ready to put the tree up."

In the kitchen, he pointed to their spots at the table. Doll forgotten, they both started in on their spaghetti. Well, Elliot wouldn't really call it spaghetti since neither of them were willing to try the sauce he'd made. He served his own plate and brought it to the table.

Beth slurped up a noodle. "When's Kate going to be here?"

Kate. He'd hoped to clean his house at least a bit before she arrived. Not that she hadn't been there before but it'd be nice to look mildly competent in front of her. It wasn't like he was trying to impress her. Hell, they were just friends and he needed to be interested in a woman the way he needed another knee to the groin

Gracie picked up her milk. "Daddy!"

"Uh. Sorry. She should be here soon. I hope you two can help with the tree," Elliot said, shaking his head with a mock look of concern.

"Why wouldn't we?" Beth asked.

"You can't help with the tree when your room looks like that," he said.

Both girls opened their mouths and looked at each other, then back at him.

Like they'd timed it, they both said, "We'll clean it."

Elliot smiled. "Okay, then. Finish up and go do it."

They chatted non-stop, faster than Elliot could keep up with, so he let his mind wander. Gina had texted approximately eight dozen times, and he was ready to change his number. Most of them read *I'm sorry. Are you mad?* No, he wasn't fucking mad because it wasn't high school. He was tired. The weary kind of tired that he knew meant he was actually, legitimately done with her bullshit. They'd been on this ride for far too long, and he hadn't liked it much after the first few tries. It was time to step all the way off, and though he hadn't wanted to go this particular route, he needed a lawyer.

The knock pulled him from his thoughts. On the way to the door, he loosened his jaw, which had gone tight at the thought of Gina.

Kate was bundled adorably, a scarf and hood hiding most of her face. Her gloved hands were in a prayer-like position, her fingers against her lips. She was bouncing on the balls of her feet and it made him laugh.

"Cold?"

She stomped her feet on his front steps, shook herself, and stepped in. He closed the door, inhaling the freshness of the snow and the subtle scent of vanilla that came with Kate.

"I'm pretty sure my lips are frozen," she said, pulling off her gloves.

Elliot pictured warming her perfect lips with his own. She yanked the scarf from around her face and neck like it was attacking her and his eyes zeroed in her mouth, apparently for too long.

"Elliot?"

She was looking at him with her flushed face and full lips, and his heart wouldn't calm the hell down. What was wrong with him? This was Kate. They were friends. Had been friends for a long time.

She poked his shoulder with one finger. "Elliot…phone home."

His eyes snapped up to see humor lighting her eyes. "Sorry. Lost my train of thought."

"Oh, I thought you were trying to figure out the movie reference."

When she shrugged out of her coat, he took it and hung it up in the entryway closet. And because he needed to prove to himself that he was just overtired and *not* falling for Kate, he gave her shoulder a brotherly shove. But the spark that sailed up his arm from the contact, zapping his heart, did *not* feel brotherly.

"It was one movie. I could top you any time with trivia."

She walked ahead of him into the kitchen, like she'd been there a dozen times before, and he followed her easy laughter.

"You're on. You'll lose, but you're on."

Before he could reply, or admit to himself that the competitive tone of her voice turned him on, the girls came running in.

"Kate!" Beth and Grace both latched onto her waist, arms flying around her.

Kate giggled along with the girls' enthusiasm as she squeezed them tight.

"Hey! My favorite twins," she said.

Both of his daughters giggled wildly, like Kate was funnier than all of their favorite shows and Elliot's heart clutched hard. He inhaled sharply.

Kate looked over her shoulder at him, her blue eyes sparkling. "You okay?"

Elliot waited for the pinching feeling to subside before nodding. "I'm good. Should we get started? I pulled out my decorations."

"Daddy, you don't have that many," Beth said, releasing Kate.

"Fear not, little one. I've brought treasures from the Aarons house," Kate said, bending down to tap Beth's nose.

When she straightened, she looked at Elliot and tilted her head. "Said treasures are in my car. When I told my mom you didn't have much, she went a little crazy packing up stuff she doesn't really use."

Elliot didn't know whether to smile or groan. The Aarons did nothing halfway. By the time he'd dragged in the two huge plastic bins from Kate's family, she and the girls had settled in the living room. Christmas music played from Kate's phone through his docking station, filling the room, and Elliot, with a festive spirit. He'd put the artificial tree together earlier, standing it in one corner of the living room.

Elliot stood in the large rounded archway that separated the living room from the kitchen and watched as Kate sat cross-legged, holding the doll of discord in her hands.

"This would actually be a pretty easy doll to make. I could do that and then you'd have two, but would you still fight over this one?" Kate asked.

Beth and Grace stared at each other a moment and Elliot smiled at their ability to communicate without talking. Kate looked over their heads and grinned, and a spark of desire burst through him so unexpectedly it stole his breath.

"We'd share them both and wouldn't fight," Beth said.

Kate nodded. "Okay. I'll make you another."

Elliot didn't know what made him happier, or more surprised, that she understood why they needed one each or that she was willing to take the time to do something so sweet for his girls.

As they unpacked Christmas ornaments, ribbons, and other tree trimmings, Kate told the girls stories of her family's holidays. The girls spent more time playing with the mini nativity set they'd found than they did helping with the tree. While he and Kate worked together to string lights, Elliot settled into a quiet kind of contentment he wasn't familiar with.

He plugged the lights into the power bar. "How was the family reunion?"

Kate shrugged. It didn't suit her. She was usually confident and sure where her family was concerned, but at the moment, she looked more lost in thought than he'd been.

"Everyone was there and I thought, wow, they all got together for brunch to welcome me home."

Elliot waited, but she stared intently at a shiny cylindrical-shaped ornament she held.

"That's nice," he said.

Her eyes met his for only a second before she busied herself with hanging the decoration.

"Except it turns out that Char, Luke, and their girls are actually staying with my parents. They were doing a kitchen remodel and some pipes burst."

"Right. I think Alex said something about that. I forgot. Still, I'm sure they were all happy to be there when you got home."

Beth and Grace curled up on the couch with a couple of books they found in one of the bins. Elliot smiled over at them before returning his focus to Kate.

"Yeah. It was nice, but not what I expected. I just felt…out of the loop, you know? It made me think of how hard I was on Lucy when she came home a couple years ago and tried to just jump back into all of our lives. I gave her a hard time and now I'm in the same spot." She gave a sad laugh that made Elliot's chest ache. "Only with nowhere to stay."

Elliot froze in the act of picking up a weird looking Santa ornament. "What?"

"Char's family is using up the rooms at my parents' place and they had to move a bunch of their stuff so they're storing it at Lucy and

Alex's."

She shrugged again. Elliot hung the Santa at the back of the tree where it would dance in the window. He walked around to stand beside her.

"You can crash here," he said.

She looked up at him and his heart pinched again at the melancholy he saw in the depth of her eyes. "That's sweet, but I need a place to live, not crash. I mean, I didn't want to stay with my parents anyway. But I thought I would for a few days at least."

Her smile came back like it had never been hiding and she patted his chest with one hand, right over his heart.

"Don't worry. After a couple nights on my parents' couch, I need a real bed. I've got some friends I can stay with. That's the good thing about coming home, right?"

She turned back to the decorations lying on the table and picked up another.

Kate looked over at the girls. "You girls going to help us?"

Beth yawned and Grace snuggled into the corner of the couch. "In a minute," Beth said. Gracie's eyes were half closed. Elliot knew he'd be carrying them both to bed.

With the hum of Christmas music setting the tone, Kate and Elliot finished decorating the tree using a combination of his ornaments and ones from her family. It was peaceful and Elliot realized he'd never felt the sense of calm with another woman that he did in Kate's presence. Growing up, his parents had been anything but calm and the holidays were no different than any other day. Doing something so traditional with Kate, to whom such activities clearly mattered, made it feel almost sentimental. He enjoyed being with her. The girls liked, no, they loved her the way kids do so freely. And she needed a place to stay. He watched her as they worked, trying not to be obvious about looking at her and probably failing if the number of times she scrunched her face quizzically at him was anything to go by.

He told himself that his attraction wouldn't get in the way of the idea he was about to bring up. In fact, if she said yes, it would put her firmly in the "no fly" zone. Kate tucked away the ornaments they didn't use, setting the lid on the container and snapping it closed. Elliot turned just as she stretched, her shirt riding up enough that he could see the smooth skin of her stomach. His fingers actually tingled—itched—with the desire to touch her and that was not the only part of his body she stirred.

Don't do it. It was probably a bad idea all around. But it was also one that would solve both of their pressing problems. *And bring up a ton of others.*

The girls had fallen asleep, and Kate was watching them wistfully. Elliot stepped closer to her and wondered if he'd imagined the tremor that went through her body when he came near.

"Stay," he said. *Idiot. Fucking idiot. Alex is going to kick your ass.*

Kate frowned. "What?"

Taking her hand, he pulled her through his now-very-festive living room and into the kitchen. She didn't pull her hand away, even when he turned her so they were facing. His chest was too crowded with emotions he couldn't name to remember to let it go. So he held tight, their fingers linking.

"I need someone to watch the girls. You need a place to live. If you stay, it fixes both of those things," he said.

Out loud, the idea didn't sound half as crazy as it felt. Maybe that was because, logistically, it was a good idea. Emotionally and physically, it might turn him inside out.

"Elliot, what are you talking about? You want me to babysit your kids?"

Her tone was just shy of insulted and he pulled his hand from hers and took a step away. When he turned back, she had one dark eyebrow arched. God, the woman had a killer face. It sucked him in, made his suggestion seem the height of stupid. He wanted to trace the curve of her jaw with his fingers and let his lips follow the path. He squeezed his eyes shut for a second; just a second to pull himself together.

"Okay. Listen, I was looking at the cost of care for the girls. It's crazy. But I can't give up my job, obviously. I work different shifts, which doesn't match up with regular daycare hours, even if what we need is mostly after-school care. You have things you want to do that don't require a nine-to-five position, right?"

Kate leaned against the counter, her eyebrows and the rest of her more relaxed. "Okay. That's true."

She hadn't said no. He kept going. "You can do what you need to do around my hours. I'll pay you to care for the girls and you'll have a place to live. I won't have to worry when I have night shifts or early morning shifts and you won't have to worry about finding a place."

Pacing his kitchen, he realized the idea was solid. Daycare *was* expensive. He *was* worried about finding a place where the girls could go at the crack of dawn and stay through the night. He had a hard enough time leaving them with their mother. Leaving them with a stranger could weigh him down so heavily, he might be distracted at work. Elliot wanted the girls and he wanted them full time. He was about to fight for them and that meant he had to show he was doing everything he could to give them the best life possible.

"Elliot, are you serious?"

He closed the distance between them. "I am. If you think about it, it's a really good solution for both of us."

Kate pulled her bottom lip between her teeth and Elliot's stomach tightened uncomfortably. He ignored it, mostly.

"I can't let you pay me to watch your kids."

"Why not?"

Now she paced. "Because they're your kids. We're friends. We help each other out."

"Sure, if I needed you to watch them for a night. But this is different. I have to have someone come here to make it work with my schedule. I want someone I can trust. Someone I like and get along with, who won't drive me crazy. Someone who cares about the girls and is great with them. I'm going to have to pay to have someone regardless but I don't want them with just anyone."

When she went for a third lap of pacing his kitchen, he grabbed her arm and pulled her closer. She looked down to where his hand encircled her wrist. He let go quickly, like he'd touched fire.

"Elliot, this is crazy."

"Maybe. But tell me what would work out better for both of us."

Kate's expression softened and the air in Elliot's lungs felt stale. She stared at him, and he forgot to breathe.

"It's a bad idea," she said.

"Kate. It's a great idea." Now that he'd said it aloud, he wanted her. *No.* He wanted her to say yes.

"I don't know that it could be long term," she said.

His heart leapt, jumped like a diver from the high board. "Even if it's temporary, it'll be better than what they're used to and give us both a chance to straighten our lives out a little."

"You do need some straightening out," she said, poking him in the stomach.

He grabbed her finger, closing his hand around her smaller one. "Who better than one of the Aarons girls to help me get my life organized?"

She did the thing with her lips and teeth again, and Elliot nearly groaned. He would not convince her by drooling over her, and if she was going to live in his house, he'd have to get over the attraction that seemed amplified in the quiet darkness of the kitchen.

"Elliot, on paper, this sounds ideal. But I really don't know that it's a good idea."

His heart screeched to a halt. "Why?"

When her eyes went soft and her body shifted closer, his heart revved up once again. Their combined breaths seemed loud, almost echoing in his ears.

Kate took a deep breath and let it out. "Look at me and tell me you don't feel the heat between us. The attraction. How long do you think we can ignore that if I'm living in the same house?"

Shit. On one hand, it was good to know he hadn't been seeing something that wasn't there—his instincts were still highly intact. She wanted him every bit as much as he wanted her. But they also had bigger goals, more important agendas that could suffer if she said no. She was looking at him now and in her eyes, he saw a reflection of what he felt. The depth of that feeling was a surprise, and damn humbling. But since the day he'd held his girls in his arms for the first time, he'd stopped putting himself first. Kate was on the verge of saying yes and he didn't want anything to stand in the way. He needed her. *They* needed her. More than that, he wanted it to be her. Wanted her to be someone who touched his girls' lives.

Looking Kate straight in the eyes, he did something he hated. He lied.

"Kate, I'm sorry if I gave you the wrong impression. Shit. I feel like a jackass now," he said. It physically hurt, like being struck with an open palm, to look at her while he said the words.

"What?" She stepped back.

"We're friends, that's all. I'm really, truly sorry if I've made you think otherwise. And of course I understand if you can't do this because, well, because you feel…differently for me."

He rubbed the back of his neck, his stomach turning in on itself.

Kate's eyes widened and she gave a high-pitched, short laugh. "What? No. It's not uncomfortable. Of course we're friends. Wow. Don't apologize," she said, her words coming fast. "I don't even know why I said that. I don't…I don't have feelings for you and of course, I didn't think you had them for me. God. I'm such an idiot. I'm so sorry. Well. At least my face is now the right shade to blend in with your Christmas decorations."

Fuck. He hated himself. "I didn't mean to make this awkward."

She shook her head too fast. "No. You didn't. This is…you know what? It's an excellent idea. You're absolutely right. We are friends. Nothing more. I adore your girls and I like you. As a friend. I need money, you need a nanny."

"Kate."

She shook her head again and when she spoke, her words were tight, like a noose wrapping around his heart.

"Elliot, I would love to work for you. I can't promise a long-term commitment, but you're right. For now, it is a perfect solution for both of us."

They stared at each other, both digesting the words. Electric energy hummed between them, more powerful because he knew, as a man and a cop, that she was as full of it as he was. He stepped forward and held out his hand.

"You're hired."

Kate looked down at it then slid her palm against his. *Fucking electric.*

"Perfect. Absolutely perfect, boss."

Chapter Eight

Kate's phone shook in her hand. Correction. It was her hand shaking. Because she was a complete idiot. Her breath refused to pull all the way into her lungs and the short, quick bursts of air were nearly as loud as her heartbeat. She typed out a text to her sisters.

> **Kate: I've solved one of life's most pressing questions. You can both thank me now.**
>
> **Char: Why men get to pee standing up?**
>
> **Lucy: Is there really a G-spot?**

She knew they'd make her laugh. They'd pull her out from the murky waters of humiliation and tell her she was overreacting.

> **Kate: You cannot, in fact, die of embarrassment. I tested that theory to the absolute limit and am sad to say that when you reach the threshold of shame, you do not go up in fire or sink into the depths of hell or fall lifeless to the floor.**

> Char: This ought to be good. Tell us more. Where are you, anyway?
>
> Lucy: Wait, let me get my wine before you give us all the details.

Or maybe they wouldn't. Maybe they'd just make her feel worse. But the embarrassment was still eating a hole in her stomach so she needed to share it.

> Kate: You both suck.
>
> Char: So? Tell us anyway.
>
> Lucy: I'm back. Tell us. And yeah, where are you?

Kate stopped pacing the guest room Elliot had said would be hers and stared at her phone. What was wrong with them? Had no one heard her? More importantly, had no one listened?

> Kate: I told you—all of you—I was going to Elliot's to help with decorating the tree. Thanks for listening. I could be dead somewhere and you wouldn't even know.
>
> Char: But you already said you didn't die of embarrassment even though you wanted to. So since you didn't, tell us what happened?
>
> Lucy: Did you see Elliot shirtless and drool all over yourself?
>
> Kate: Do you want to know or not?
>
> Char: Lucy, knock it off or she won't tell us.

Lucy: Bossy.

Char: Brat.

Kate: GUYS!

Kate sank into the softness of the double bed as a knock came. She jumped back up, tucked her phone in her pocket, and opened the door. Elliot stood in the threshold.

"Hey." He rolled in her suitcase, which, ever the gentleman, he'd grabbed for her from the back of her mom's car. He ran a hand through his dark hair. "You need anything? I just tucked in the girls. I work at six tomorrow."

Kate shook her head. "Nope. I'm good. Great. Really tired though." She faked a yawn and Elliot raised one eyebrow in response.

"Okay. You sure you're okay?"

Smiling so wide her cheeks hurt, Kate nodded. *Damnit, stop nodding like a bobble head doll.* "I'm good. Really. It's okay if I take the girls out tomorrow? I'll need to grab some of my stuff from my parents' and then I promised them I'd take them shopping."

Elliot shoved both of his hands into the pockets of his jeans. Kate kept her eyes up, though they really wanted to travel down the length of him.

"It's fine. You really don't have to do that though. The shopping. We can all go when I get home tomorrow. After dinner."

"Nope. This is a girls-only trip."

"Okay."

She stepped back from the door and he started to turn away. When he turned back, Kate's breath caught in her throat. Painfully.

"Kate?"

"Mmm?"

"I'm glad you're here."

She could only nod. Shutting the door, she leaned her forehead against it for a moment, then pulled out her phone again.

Several texts popped up from her sisters.

> **Lucy: Sorry.**
>
> **Char: Sorry, honey. Go ahead.**
>
> **Lucy: Where are you? We said sorry! Come back.**
>
> **Char: Come on. Don't be like that…come back.**
>
> **Lucy: Kate Marie Aarons!**
>
> **Kate: Stop it! I was talking to Elliot for a minute. He offered me a perfect solution to my no-job, no-place-to-live issue.**
>
> **Char: Oh, Kate, I feel terrible. Honestly, we can get the kids to bunk with us in Lucy's old room, you take yours.**
>
> **Lucy: Let her finish.**
>
> **Kate: It's okay. I now have both a job and a place to live. I'm going to be a live-in nanny for Beth and Grace.**
>
> **Lucy: Okay.…**
>
> **Char: You're going to be a babysitter?**
>
> **Lucy: Char. Bitchy.**

Kate had said the same. She had a degree in social work and had just finished an internship at a top New York fashion house. She'd even won the coveted best intern award six months ago. And now, she was lying back on a paisley print duvet in the house of a man she more than lusted after, waiting for the shame to fade far enough into the back of her mind that she could just find the whole thing funny.

> **Char: Lucy, practical. She wants to open a dress shop and eat. Babysitting is not exactly a stepping stone for that.**
>
> **Kate: Why did I text you guys?**
>
> **Lucy: Sorry.**
>
> **Char: Sorry.**
>
> **Kate: It is a good stepping stone. I don't pay for rent, he'll take care of food, and he's actually offered me really decent money. I adore the girls and I can get things settled and started around his shift work. It's…kind of ideal.**
>
> **Lucy: What's the problem then?**
>
> **Char: It sounds good.**

Kate took a deep breath, glanced at the door of the bedroom she'd be using as her own, then looked back at her phone.

> **Kate: Before I realized what a great solution it was, I told him I didn't think it was a good idea because obviously there is a significant amount of heat between us and living under the same roof would**

only lead to trouble.

Char: The yummiest kind of trouble.

Lucy: He's a bit old for you. And has two kids. Not exactly a fling.

Char: Now who's bitchy?

Lucy: I'm just saying. She has a lot going on. Starting up her own business isn't exactly easy, and Elliot's got baggage in the shape of Gina.

Char: True.

Kate: Are you done?

Char: Sorry.

Lucy: Sorry.

Kate: He informed me that he wasn't sure if he gave me mixed signals but he thought of me as no more than a friend, and whatever heat I was referring to was clearly only on my part.

Silence. Sitting alone in the quiet of the sparsely decorated spare room, Kate's cheeks heated again. She could hear Elliot puttering around down the hall and another wave of regret shook her shoulders. He was supposed to be going to bed. *Do not think about him and bed.*

Kate: HELLO?

Lucy: Sorry. I just died of embarrassment for you.

Char: And instead of fleeing the country so you

never had to see him again, you chose to move in?

Kate growled at her phone. She tossed it beside her and then got up, stripped down to her tank top and underwear, and crawled between the coolness of the covers. When she realized she'd forgotten the light, she got up, switched it off, groped her way back to the bed, and picked up her phone, the glow lighting the dark.

Lucy: DUDE. Be nice.

Char: 12-year-old boys say dude. Grow up.

Lucy: My brain is too sleepy to think of a good comeback. When I finally do, I'm just going to randomly insert it.

Char: That's what he said.

Despite the irritation and unrest making a home inside of her, Kate snickered.

Kate: You two are idiots and terrible sisters.

Char: But we love you.

Lucy: Usually.

Kate: I'm such a loser.

One tear leaked onto the pillow.

Lucy: NO. You are not. You are an amazing designer, a beautiful woman, and Elliot is a blind, drunken idiot.

Kate: He was sober.

Lucy: So all of the other stuff then.

Char: She's right. You're the full package. I'm sorry you're embarrassed and probably nursing hurt feelings but…it's probably for the best. Lucy is right, he does have a lot of baggage, and if you want this to work out, you do not need to be doing your boss. When it ends, it would be messy on so many different levels. So this is better.

More tears threatened, and she bit her lip to hold them off.

Lucy: I think I just died again when Char said I was right. Honey, I'm sorry. He's one guy. You've got lots going on. And you don't need to be lusting after him while you're working for him. Focus on your shop. We're going to do everything we can to help. Actually, speaking of that…remember the small coffee shop that Joy Hillier tried to start a few years back?

Char: Before she took over a foster care center in another town?

Kate: I forgot about that. What about it?

Lucy: Alex says it's available for lease. It's a good location—right on the outskirts of town.

Kate: Cool. I'll see if I can go take a look. I should go to bed. Elliot has to work tomorrow so it's officially my first day.

Lucy: Okay…you know who IS cute and available?

Kate: Don't.

Char: Who?

Kate: Stop it.

Lucy: Cam. I could set it up. Or nag Alex to help me set it up. He's so sweet!

Kate: Goodnight.

Lucy: Come on!

Char: He is really cute. Good job. No kids. No crazy ex.

All true. But Cam didn't make her stomach trip over itself like a klutzy teenager who hadn't grown into their full height yet. He didn't make Kate's heart speed up or make her want to hold her breath just so she could listen to his breathing.

Kate: I hope you both got me something insanely overpriced for Christmas. If not, there are still a few shopping days left.

Lucy: We could invite him for Christmas brunch.

Kate: I'll tell Alex you're trying to make him play matchmaker.

Lucy: You're mean.

Char: Get some sleep. Lucy, leave her alone.

Lucy: Bossy.

Kate: Jesus. Goodnight.

Lucy: Love you.

Char: Love you.

Kate: Yeah. Love you both too. Most of the time.

A shard of light filtered through the gap in the curtains. Kate closed her eyes but the memory of Elliot's pained expression as he explained her misinterpretation kept rushing through her mind. She'd been so restless, so ready to come home, so certain everything untethered in her chest and stomach would settle down in familiar surroundings. Instead, she only felt more unconnected. More alone.

"Better alone in a place you know than one you don't," she whispered into the dark. But she wasn't sure she believed herself.

Chapter Nine

Elliot was an idiot. He'd reminded himself of that several times over the past few of mornings. The first time Kate stumbled out of his guest room, looking like a sexy, sleepy siren, Elliot had lost the power of coherent thought. Her hair was mussed and her blue eyes were a little darker in the morning, a little unfocused. She wore a tank top and a pair of yoga pants that hugged her sweet curves, and Elliot had nearly spilled his coffee when she'd tumbled into the kitchen.

He'd mumbled unintelligibly about getting to work and left without his travel mug, which meant that by the time he rolled into work, he was still mildly turned on and greatly in need of caffeine.

This morning was no different. He came face to face with Alex before he could reach the coffee pot.

"Morning. You getting any sleep?" Alex said.

Elliot met Alex's gaze, telling himself there was no way his boss could know the thoughts that had crowded his mind for the whole drive.

"Morning."

Alex arched an eyebrow. The phone rang and Dolores, their front desk receptionist answered in a sing-song voice that was both two high and too loud.

Elliot continued to hold Alex's gaze as the Chief of Angel's Lake Police sipped his cup of coffee. Was he salivating? The staring contest seemed necessary. If Elliot broke away first, it would confirm he'd thought of tumbling his new nanny into bed.

"You okay, Peters?" Alex asked.

"Yup. Thanks again for the extra days. I appreciate it."

"No problem. You get everything sorted with Gina?"

Elliot grimaced. He couldn't handle talk of his ex without more caffeine. "For now. Enough."

"Heard you have a sexy new nanny," Alex said, lowering his mug to the counter he was leaning on.

"No! I mean, yes. I have a nanny. Kate. Kate's my nanny," Elliot said, choking on his own words. "Not my nanny. She's watching the girls. There's nothing sexy about it."

Alex looked like he was trying very hard not to laugh. Elliot nearly growled and decided that things would only get worse if he didn't do something about the coffee situation. He turned, poured himself a cup and took a huge gulp. He refilled the cup and walked back over to Alex. Dolores smiled and waved at him. Off the phone now, she was singing along with a pop radio station that made Elliot want to stab his ears.

"So, just to make sure I'm hearing you right, you do not find Kate sexy?"

Elliot choked on his coffee. It took him a minute to regain his breath. All the while, Alex watched with far too much amusement.

Finally, he spoke around his raw throat. "Kate and I are friends.

Nothing more."

"Hmm." Alex nodded his head once, picked up his coffee cup, and filled it. When he turned back, he clapped Elliot on the shoulder. "Just keep in mind you hurt her, I can't fire you, but I can make you wish I would."

Elliot stared at his coffee. "Noted."

And once again, he called himself an idiot.

Angel's Lake wasn't exactly a hub of crime, but it kept the six deputies and their chief busy enough. By the time Elliot pulled into his driveway at nearly seven, he was drained. He'd dealt with shoplifting kids—always a problem at Christmas—two accidents, traffic duty when the lights coming into town stopped working, and a domestic dispute.

He wanted a hot shower, a cold beer, and some cuddles from his girls. He'd forgotten to talk to Kate about meals so he hoped she'd fed them.

When he came in, the house was way too quiet. The table was clear but the kitchen smelled like garlic and other spices, and his stomach rumbled noisily. He set his keys, wallet, and cell phone on the counter as Kate came tiptoeing into the kitchen.

She startled when she saw him then put a finger to her lips. He watched her, amused, as she came closer.

"I'm hunting elves. If I find them before the timer rings, they have to take a bath with no fussing," she whispered.

She smelled like flowers. He didn't know the names of most flowers, but whatever one was making Kate smell like spring was his new favorite. He clenched his fingers so he wouldn't reach out and touch her.

"What happens if the timer goes and you don't find them? Do they just have to be smelly elves?"

She winked at him and it was like sending a shock straight to his gut. She pointed to the table, and though he hadn't noticed earlier, he saw the tip of a foot underneath a pushed-in chair.

"I'll find them," she whispered.

Elliot watched, fascinated, as she tiptoed past the table one way then the other. He heard the giggle, so he knew Kate did too, but still she paced. Then she sighed loud enough that he would have heard her in another room.

"I give up. These must be magic invisible elves," Kate said. She pulled out a chair and flopped into it. Both of the girls squealed and Kate dropped to her knees. "Found you!"

A chorus of giggling and tickling ensued and Elliot wasn't sure who was sillier, or cuter, his daughters or their nanny. How could a grown woman act so silly and still be so incredibly alluring? *Because she's making your daughters laugh and enjoying it.* He hadn't known that could be attractive.

"Hi, Daddy!" Beth came out from under the table and rushed to him. He bent and picked her up as Grace followed.

"Hi, Daddy," she said.

He leaned over and boosted Grace up into his arms as well. "How are my two favorite girls?"

"We're good. But we gotta have a bath," Beth said.

Grace ran her hand over his jaw then nuzzled into him. His heart flip-flopped. "Good thing. You smell like elves."

The girls laughed. He gave them a squeeze, kissed each of their cheeks, and set them down.

"Should we feed you before you have a bath?" he asked.

Grace took Beth's hand. "We already ate. Will you read our stories?"

Elliot locked eyes with Kate. "I didn't mean for you to have to cook each night too. Sorry. Thanks for getting them fed, again. I'll give them a bath and put them to bed. I meant to grab groceries so you wouldn't have to. We can sort some of that stuff out after they're down for the night."

Kate smiled and pushed the chair back in. "Sure, we can talk later. Dinner is in the oven. I'll get them into the bath. You unwind, have something to eat, and then you'll be ready for stories."

Without waiting for an answer, she followed the girls, who were already headed for the bath. Elliot stood in his kitchen, staring after them. Never mind magic elves, Elliot had found himself a magical woman. She was still smiling at the end of another twelve-hour day, she'd cooked him dinner three nights in a row, his daughters were happy, and his house smelled like a combination of excellent food and sexy female. What the hell was he supposed to do with that? He couldn't have guessed how awesome it would feel to come home to his girls and Kate, laughing and smiling. It refreshed him, and as he zapped his plate of roast pork and potatoes in the microwave, he wondered how he could make it last without messing it up.

Elliot tucked Grace into her bed, which was next to Beth's. Kissing her on the forehead, he breathed in the scent of her freshly washed hair.

"I missed you guys today. Was it fun hanging out with Kate?"

He leaned over and kissed Beth, sitting down beside her on the edge of her bed.

"Kate's funny. And nice. And she smells pretty," Beth said, reaching out for Elliot's hand.

"She is." Very funny. Extremely nice. Way too pretty.

"We got you a Christmas present today. Kate helped us pick it out, but it's not a puppy," Grace said, sitting up and taking a drink out of the glass beside her bed.

Elliot choked on a laugh and made a mental note to thank Kate later.

"Let's get settled with us first and we'll see about puppies in the future."

"Beth and me wanna get Kate something for Christmas. She really wants a puppy," Grace said.

"A puppy is a pretty big gift, sweetie. But we can definitely get her something. We need to go shopping anyway so we'll do it in a few days. I missed a bit of work coming to get you guys so I've got to work for the next four days."

He stood up, walked to the door, and hit the switch on the wall. Their night table lamps had star cutouts, which created shapes that danced across the ceiling and walls.

"I love you girls."

"Love you, Daddy," they said together, then giggled.

He stared at them a moment longer and went to find the third best thing that had happened to him. Kate was more than a godsend; she was a damn miracle worker. He knew she couldn't stay long, but he wondered how the heck his home—and his life—would run without her. He'd had the girls for weeks at a time before and it had felt like a juggling act. Today felt like a well-rehearsed skit he wouldn't mind performing again and again. Indefinitely.

Don't go there. Look how well forever worked out last time, Peters.

The thought was stuck in his head as he walked through the kitchen, snagged them both a beer from his fridge, and found her in the living room. The lights from the tree glowed, even from the hall. The peaceful scene of Kate sketching on his couch stopped him in his tracks.

The flames of the gas fireplace danced, sending shadows over the softness of Kate's body curled into the corner of the cushions. Her dark hair fell across her cheeks, curtaining her view of him. His heart beat like a drum, heavy and loud, then increased in tempo, like a marching band building up to the crescendo. He couldn't move. What the fuck was he scared of? He'd liked her since the day he'd met her. Every woman was *not* Gina. No other woman was Kate. She didn't run and she didn't hide. She was strong and fearless and so goddamn sweet it made him ache.

He must have made a noise because her head snapped up and her eyes locked on his. She gave a small gasp of surprise that echoed in the quiet. The neck of the beer bottles were numbing his fingers but still, he stood staring at her, lost in her.

His voice was rough when he spoke. "What are you working on?"

Eyes not leaving his, she turned the book and he saw two dresses, similar but different. She was designing clothes for his girls. *Fuck.* He was sunk.

Chapter Ten

Kate's hands trembled slightly as she held the sketchbook so Elliot could see. Was he even looking at the adorable gowns she'd drawn for the girls? His eyes darted to her sketchbook quickly and then locked back on hers. What the actual hell? She'd been mortified for days now, her nights practically sleepless, every time she'd thought of their conversation. She'd made sure to be in the middle of something or unable to talk when he came home at night. How could she face him when she'd made such a fool of herself?

It was like being naïve —and wrong—was her new hobby. She'd been sure New York was for her. Wrong. She had thought she'd had a real connection with Darby. Stupid. She'd thought her family would weep with joy at her return. Not so much. When she'd been wrong about Elliot's feelings, the last of her confidence in her own ability to be sure about anything had turned tail and fled.

Now he was looking at her and everything inside of her was going haywire like circuits being blown. He was *not* looking at her like a goddamn friend. She might be wrong about a lot of things and she might have no idea where the hell she'd go from here, but she could read him, better than he thought.

The air pumped with tension and their combined breathing. He didn't blink as she set the sketchbook on the couch and rose. The Christmas lights played tag on the wall, blinking on and off. Her heart wouldn't settle. Instead, it urged her forward. Two beers hung loosely in his grip and she watched his jaw tighten, but still, his eyes held hers. The closer she got and the more she could see the hunger in them, the surer she became. She hadn't been wrong. *God* that mattered. She needed to feel sure about something. And she was sure that Elliot Peters wanted her every bit as much as she wanted him.

When she was within touching distance, she stopped, held his gaze. *Don't do this. Don't.* But she had to; she needed to know.

With another small step, the front of her body brushed his. He inhaled sharply and closed his eyes, breathing through his nose. Kate's heart smiled.

"You're a liar," she whispered.

He opened his eyes. "Excuse me?"

"Friends don't lie to friends," she said.

The bottles clinked together. Neither of them moved.

"Kate."

"Tell me again," she said, feeling stronger, surer. Braver.

His eyes darted to her lips. "Tell you what?"

Did Elliot Peters' voice just squeak? Power and desire surged through Kate and she felt like…like herself again. Not lost in a city that really never slept. She felt like she had when she'd been in charge of rebuilding the rec center in Angel's Lake a couple years ago: certain that only good could come from her actions.

"Tell me you only have feelings for me as a friend," she said. Her fingers itched to touch him.

With a deep sigh, Elliot leaned down, put the beers on the small side table.

When he stood straight again, he tunneled his hands into her hair, his eyes locked onto hers. She pressed her hands to his chest, unable to look away as his mouth came toward hers. Right before their lips touched, he sighed again, filling her with the sweetness of his breath.

"I lied."

And then it didn't matter because his mouth was on hers, tasting, testing, and teasing. His fingers tightened in her hair as one hand snaked down, pressing against the small of her back, and bringing her so close that she became part of him. It was like being absorbed, surrounded, by warmth and tenderness. And a passion so strong it had claws. Her hands moved restlessly, up around his neck then back down to the hem of his T-shirt. She found skin and her stomach tumbled, like when she'd spun around too many times as a young girl. She didn't want the spinning to stop.

Elliot boosted her up, and Kate wrapped her legs around his waist, moaned when his lips and the gentle scruff of a few days' growth scraped along her neck. When tremors coursed through her body, over her skin, sanity knocked lightly. Lifting her head, she looked down at him and cupped his jaw in her hands.

She had to ask; she couldn't be someone else's mistake. "Do we want to talk about this?"

Elliot turned, with her clutching him, and walked toward his bedroom. "We'll talk after."

He shut the door with his foot, holding her with one strong arm like a vice as he turned the lock. Padding toward the bed, Kate thought that if looks could burn, she'd go up in flames.

With more gentleness than she expected, he lowered her to the bed, his eyes doing more to consume her than his roaming hands. When he reached for the buttons, his fingers grazing her breasts, she stopped him. His eyes went to hers again.

"Just tell me you won't think it's a mistake," she whispered.

Elliot's eyes flashed with surprise and his hands came up to cradle her jaw. He leaned down and brushed his nose along the bridge of hers, kissing her cheek.

"Kate. You could never be a mistake. You're perfection," he said, holding her gaze.

She knew, because she'd come to know him, that he was waiting for her go ahead, for her to be sure. So she could see the truth. So she could *feel* it. And believe it.

She placed her hands on his and slid them back to where he'd had them. Elliot grinned but before her lips could curve into a full smile in return, he'd erased the distance between them.

Elliot's fingers traced up and down her side, along her bare skin. His warm breath was in her hair, on her neck, and she was snuggled against him, certain she'd never felt so at home. It was like driving around in circles, continuously looking for a better parking spot. Finally, one opens up and confirms the waiting, the extra effort, was completely worth it. Kate felt like that now—like *this* was where she was meant to be. There was no other spot in which she'd fit so perfectly. And it scared the hell out of her because her life was a precariously balanced, over-stacked tower of blocks: any quick movements and it could come tumbling down.

"What are you thinking?" he whispered.

"I was wondering how I missed this. Wondering if it's been here the whole time, simmering between us, and I've just been oblivious."

Elliot turned her so she was looking up at him. His fingers went to her face and traced along her hairline down to her jawbone.

"I think, to some extent, it's always been here, but neither of us were in a position to act on it," he said.

It felt true. She'd been attracted to him from the beginning, but there was school, the rec center, and then New York. Now she was home. Was the time right? Was there ever a right time?

"Are we in that position now?"

Elliot laughed, his breath fanning her ear and his body leaning into hers. "I think we're in a great position now." His palm flattened on her stomach and trailed up. She would have laughed but his mouth found hers again.

Pulling back only far enough to speak, he whispered, "Now we're here. You're in my bed. And it feels like it's exactly where you belong. With me and the girls. I thought it was the wrong time—you just getting home, me with the girls. I told you I wasn't attracted to you because I wanted you here so badly. I thought I could just…push this down. But now, now I don't know what to do with everything I'm feeling."

He was, quite possibly, the sweetest man she'd ever met. Her heart was pulsating, beaming from his words. Kate put her arms around his neck, drawing him down so she could bury her face just under his ear, so she could hug him and hold him tight. His arms wrapped around her and they stayed like that, perfectly surrounded by each other. She couldn't remember the last time she'd felt so free.

"This is where I want to be," she whispered into the quiet.

Chapter Eleven

Kate snuck back to her own bed around four in the morning. Even after she'd curled under the covers, sleep hadn't been easy. Not with the sexy play-by-play of the hours before looping in her mind. By the time she got up at seven, Elliot had gone to work. He'd left a note by the coffee maker: *Ready to go, just press start. Thought you might be tired ;)*

She was exhausted, she thought, listening to the coffee drip with a silly smile on her lips, a delicious and delightful kind of tired. Beth padded into the kitchen carrying the rag doll she and her sister shared. How ridiculous was it to buy only one gift for two girls and make them share it? Kate was almost finished sewing the second one. She'd make sure it got done today.

"Good morning," Kate said.

Beth shuffled right to her and buried her head in Kate's stomach, working her way further into Kate's heart at the same time. She put her arms around the little girl and kissed her head.

"Want pancakes?"

Beth nodded against Kate's pajamas. Grace came in looking much more awake than her twin.

"I want pancakes," she said, joining the hug.

So they made pancakes. Together. Kate tried not to think too much about how perfect it was to make breakfast with the girls in Elliot's kitchen. She hadn't even known she could want something like this—whatever it was—because she'd been chasing a different dream. If she got her Christmas wish, both dreams would be hers. But first, she had some work to do.

When the girls finished dressing, she grabbed their coats and boots.

"Put em' on, ladies. We've got errands to run," Kate said.

"Where we going?" Grace asked.

She'd finally pressed send on her application for a loan. "There's a store I want to rent so I can sell pretty dresses. We're going to go check it out."

Beth groaned. "I don't want to."

Kate stopped. It couldn't all be holiday songs and cheer, she supposed. "We won't be that long, sweetie."

Beth pulled on her boots while she complained. "But Tara gets to go to the Christmas party at the rec center. How come we can't go?"

Kate looked at Grace while she tied her own boots. "Who's Tara?"

Pulling her jacket on, Grace frowned. "Beth's best friend other than me."

"What time is this so-called party?" Kate helped Beth zip her jacket when it got stuck.

"I don't know but it's going to be really fun. Can we go?"

Kate grabbed her jacket and pulled it on, then looked up the number of the rec center's front desk.

A very musical voice answered, nearly singing, "How can I help you?"

"Hi. I'm just curious, do you have a children's Christmas party happening today?" Kate looked at the girls who watched her, eyes wide. Listening to the woman tell her about the festivities, she exaggerated her own responses to make the girls smile. "You *do*? And what time is it at? Can anyone attend? Right. Thank you. Merry Christmas to you, too."

When she put her phone in her purse, she pretended to go about zipping up her jacket, ignoring the girl's stares. Finally they laughed, filling the kitchen with their own brand of music.

"Kate!" they chorused.

Kate looked up in mock surprise. "Yes? Oh. Did you want to know about the Christmas party?"

"Yes," Beth said. Grace nodded.

"It starts at one o'clock, which means," Kate said, checking her watch, "we have enough time to go check out the shop, stop by and visit my mom, who makes the best cookies ever, and still get to the party in time."

Both girls walked to the car smiling and laughing. Kate wondered how Gina could let go of these moments. But as sad as it was, Kate felt selfishly grateful she was getting to share in them, to be part of their lives. And Elliot's.

Kate collapsed onto a plastic chair next to Lucy. Beth and Grace ditched their coats, rubbed noses, and made oddly loud cooing noises at

Emma, then dashed off to the cookie decorating station. Unbelievable. How did they still have energy? Kate had thought checking out the store space, stopping by the bank, and running a few errands would be simple. But nothing was simple when Grace forgot her doll, Beth was thirsty, or they both had to pee—at different times.

Lucy let Emma toddle around with the other kids, even though she was younger than most of the children playing in the open gym. Stations were set up around the festive space: cookies, coloring, gingerbread making, and ornament decorating.

Lucy looked Kate up and down. "You okay?"

Kate glanced sideways. "Uh, I think so. I can't believe how tired I am from running around this morning." She fanned her face with the flyer she'd been given at the door. Her hair was falling out of its ponytail, and she'd spilled coffee down the front of her sweater. Lucy, however, looked radiant. Her dark hair glistened and her cheeks were still bright from the cold outside. Emma gave her mom a board book.

"Read," Emma said.

Kate smiled. Grace and Beth were giggling wildly over their cookies. "I'll read to you," she said.

She held her hand out for the book and Emma turned and stared at her a moment as if judging her suitability for the task. Then she slapped the book into Kate's palm and wiggled her way onto her lap. Kate's heart clutched impossibly hard as she inhaled the fresh scent of baby shampoo.

"Nothing is ever simple with kids," Lucy said, glancing over at Beth and Grace. "But it's worth it."

Kate read a story about the different sounds animals make and Emma asked her to do it "again." After the third "again," Lucy pulled her daughter over to her lap.

"Let's go color Santa pictures," Lucy said.

Kate checked her watch and was about to go see how the girls were doing when her phone vibrated. Glancing up and seeing the twins had moved onto the coloring station themselves, Kate grabbed her phone.

> **Elliot: I seem to be unusually tired but can't stop smiling.**

Kate grinned as a sweet heaviness settled in her chest.

> **Kate: I know the feeling. We're at a Christmas party at the rec center.**

> **Elliot: Since you're technically my babysitter, how am I supposed to get a date with you?**

Kate laughed and checked on the girls again before she typed back.

> **Kate: I'm open to an afterhours date. At your house.**

> **Elliot: Sounds perfect. Give the girls a kiss for me.**

> **Kate: I will.**

> **Elliot: I'll take care of your kiss myself.**

Kate wondered if it was too much to text back "swoon." But that was definitely how she felt.

Lucy walked over, Emma fidgeting in her arms. "What's that look?"

Kate blinked and stuck her phone in her back pocket. "What look?"

Lucy grabbed Emma's coat and started wrestling her into it. Emma kept shouting "crayon," which sounded more like "crown."

"The oh-isn't-he-dreamy-I-want-some-more-look," Lucy said.

Kate's face warmed and she looked toward the twins. Lucy stood up with Emma back in her arms.

"Yeah. That's what I thought it would be like with you living with Officer Sexy Surfer," her sister said.

"Shh." Kate looked around but the kids were all engaged. Plenty of rec center employees were helping them and only a handful of parents had stuck around. They were chatting over in a corner. No one had heard, but still, her face was on fire.

"Is it a secret?"

"No, but it doesn't need to be a public announcement either." She hadn't thought that far ahead and wondered whether Elliot wanted people to know.

Lucy shook her head but amusement tipped up the corners of her mouth. Emma started squirming to get out of her mom's hold.

"I have to go. She needs a nap. Be good. Or safe. One of those. I don't know if you can do both at the same time," Lucy said.

Kate only grinned. "Pretty sure I can handle both."

She gave Emma a kiss and waved as Lucy left. She let the girls do their thing, sticking to the sidelines, and watching them enjoy each of the activities. Perhaps they could do some of their own baking the next day.

In just a few days, Elliot and his daughters had woven Kate into their lives, making her a part of something she'd never experienced in quite this way. Her mind was wandering back to the night before, so when a hand touched her shoulder, she jumped.

One of the program coordinators stood at Kate's side, her eyes suspiciously wet. Kate knew her from high school, but they hadn't hung out in the same circle.

"Hey, Cole. You okay?"

She nodded, which was at odds with the tightness around her mouth and eyes. "Yes. Sort of. Listen, it's crazy that I'm even asking you this. I'd be embarrassed or worried about offending you if I had any time for that, but I don't."

Kate half-grinned. "Sounds ominous."

Hands wringing themselves into a frenzy, Cole spoke quickly. "We've been working on a Christmas play for a while now. It's supposed to happen Christmas Eve. But our seamstress—she's also the librarian—maybe you've met her? Anyway, she broke her hand last week and we've been frantically trying to find someone else to finish what she's started." She took a deep breath in and when she exhaled, the rest of her words came with it. "And design and sew the Sugar Plum Fairy costume."

Kate felt her eyes widen. She could do some costumes; it was hardly a big deal, yet the woman looked pale, like if she squeezed her hands together any harder, she was going to cut off circulation. Kate reached out and put her hands on both of Cole's.

One of Cole's tears leaked and she pulled a hand away to brush at it. Her blond hair hung to her shoulders, and Kate thought the style suited her face. "You're a big-shot New York designer. I can't believe I'm asking you this. I'm sorry. I know you probably—"

Kate cut her off with a hand in the air. "Stop. Please. I'm hardly a big shot. Least of all in New York. I love that you're putting on a Christmas play here and I'd be happy to help."

Before Cole could express the gratitude that was written all over her face, Beth tugged on Kate's sleeve.

"I want to be in a Christmas play," she said.

Grace joined her sister, taking Beth's hand. "Me too!"

"Can we, Kate?" Beth asked.

Kate winced and looked at Cole, who kneeled down and looked at the girls. "We definitely need more fairies for the dream sequence.

Would you like to do that?"

Both girls jumped up and down, but only Beth answered. "We're perfect fairies. Can we, Kate?"

Kate looked at them, then back at the much-happier woman. "We have to check with your dad." Turning to Cole, she asked, "Is that okay? I'll talk to Elliot tonight, and if you want to drop off the costumes that have been started, I should be able to get through them fairly quick," Kate said. She paused. "How many costumes are we talking?"

"There are six dresses that still need the final stitching, a nutcracker costume that has been cut out but not stitched, and the sugar plum fairy," Cole said. She stood but glanced down at Beth and Grace who were dancing around, hand in hand. "And two back-up fairy costumes."

Kate nodded. "Okay. It's eight days until Christmas. I can sleep after, right?"

Cole's face fell, and Kate rushed forward, giving the woman a friendly hug. "I'm joking. It's fine. Drop the costumes off tonight. Give me your phone number, and I'll text you the address."

Now she smiled, all traces of tears gone. "Come on, Kate. You think there are any single women in this town that don't know where Officer Peters lives or that it hasn't spread through town, with some envy I might add, that you're living there now?"

Kate laughed. Right, of course they knew where he lived. This was Angel's Lake. It wasn't that big, and Elliot definitely stood out. In more ways than one. He was well known for pitching in around the community, even dropping in to the rec center frequently to play games of pick up ball with some of the teens. He was more than looks—he was kind and sweet. Funny and sexy. Kate's belly danced as she remembered the night before. *No time for that. But there'll be time later.*

Chapter Twelve

Elliot tried to cover his yawn, but Kate smirked as she walked back into the kitchen from the porch.

"Busted," she said, making him smile. Fuck, she just had to breathe and he'd smile.

Her arms were loaded with dresses and fabric. He took it from her and set it on the table he'd just cleared. The girls hadn't wanted to go to bed tonight, but once their heads had hit the pillows, they'd both been out. The excitement and activity of Christmas and Kate moving in with them was catching up with them.

"What's all this?" Elliot asked, running a hand down her dark hair as she inspected the fabric. He still couldn't believe she'd been in his bed the night before. Nothing in his previous experience compared to being with Kate. He'd never felt so completely connected, physically *and* emotionally to any other woman. He hadn't even known he was missing that depth of connection. He was starting to realize why nothing had worked out romantically in the past the way he'd planned, why nothing had dug in and held on: No other woman had been Kate. The thought scared him, but that didn't make it any less true.

"There's a Christmas play at the rec center, and their seamstress broke her hand," Kate said.

Elliot had been walking back to the station with coffee when that happened. "Right. Milly McCreary. I don't think I knew she was a seamstress. I know she runs the library and she slipped going up those stairs," Elliot said.

Kate's eyebrow arched. "Sometimes I forget how small this town is."

Pulling her attention from the dresses, Elliot wrapped his arms around her waist. "Hard to forget when you're here, isn't it? Speaking of which," he said, trailing off.

She'd been pressing small kisses to the underside of his jaw but when he stopped talking, she leaned back. "Speaking of which?"

Elliot's heart hammered too hard. Why the hell was he nervous? "Won't take long for this to get out." He gestured between them.

Kate's lips pursed up as she considered it. "I suppose that's okay. I mean, unless you're not okay with it. If you want to protect the girls I understand."

"Protect the girls?"

She shrugged right out of his embrace. "You know, from rumors, or if this doesn't work out. I mean, it's kind of sudden and you've just gotten them back with the intention of not letting them go again. Oh, speaking of the girls and the play—they have small parts. I hope that's okay. And I didn't tell anyone about us. I mean, Lucy, but she doesn't count. Plus, she more guessed than was told. I don't want you to feel like you have—"

Elliot's lips twitched with the need to laugh. He pressed his fingers to her mouth. *God, she's adorable.*

"I don't know what you're going to say but you should stop. First of all, we could stand still on the lawn and rumors would still fly. That's the beauty of small towns. It's not sudden when you consider we've known each other for *years* and while I never acted on it and neither did you, I've been attracted to you for every single one of them. You are by far the best female influence those girls have had, other than the other women in your family. I don't care about rumors; I care about my girls. And you." *So much about you.* He wanted to say more: How he'd never wanted to be with anyone the way he did Kate. How she made everything better. But he couldn't tell her all that he felt right now. If he gave her everything that was still waiting inside of him to be said, the emotions barrelling through him, he might scare her, or worse, push her away. The progression of his feelings was on warp speed. He'd gone from zero to ninety without blinking from the moment he'd touched his lips to hers. But she had so much going on and his life was always going to include Beth and Grace. It was a lot to spring on a woman when he hadn't even taken her out on a proper date yet.

Her chest rose and fell in deep breaths. She pulled her bottom lip between her teeth, still looking at him. Was she uncertain? Should he tell her he was one hundred and ten percent in? He'd support whatever she wanted to do—run her own boutique, design clothes from home—whatever she wanted. As long as she stayed. It was like when he embraced the idea of being done with Gina's bullshit—when he decided that he was going to firmly plant his family all in one spot and get it right—everything had settled exactly as it was supposed to. And Kate had taken root in that spot with them. Without her, it just wouldn't feel right.

"Kate?" She was killing him with her silence.

"It seems too easy," she said, her voice almost a whisper.

A smile settled in his heart as firmly as it did on his face. That was her biggest concern? "You're right." He crossed to her, took her hands, and pulled her close. "It's easy because it's supposed to be. People convince themselves it's supposed to be hard, but it shouldn't be. I mean, it will be. There'll be fights and days that just suck all the way around, but at the core, when two people care about each other, it shouldn't be hard. The relationships we've fought for? The ones that seemed too hard? Maybe they're hard because they weren't meant to last and we just didn't want to see that."

Kate watched her fingers play with the buttons on his shirt. "That's quite… philosophical."

Elliot laughed and tipped her chin up with his hand. "I wouldn't know. I slept through Philosophy 101. But I don't want you to run because it's too easy or because it's too hard. So why don't we just take what comes? Together."

She was nodding even as she went up on her tiptoes. "That sounds reasonable." Her teeth nipped at the underside of his jaw and her nose brushed up against his neck. Wrapping her arms around his neck, she gave him a gut-twistingly sweet smile. "You're a puzzle."

They breathed each other's air, their lips almost touching. "What's that supposed to mean?"

Now she giggled and the sound shot straight to his gut, making desire coil tightly inside of him. He ran his hands down to her waist, pulling her tighter as she answered.

"Nothing bad. Just, you look like a sexy surfer, you're a tough-as-steel cop, but you're soft and sweet with your girls. You're funny and thoughtful, but completely serious and hard to read sometimes. You're easygoing but like to be scheduled. You're like both sides of a coin."

His mouth touched hers, a whisper of a kiss, just a tease, then he pulled back, even though he felt her lean into him. Turning her, he walked her back to the living room in slow steps, kissing her on the way and loving the feel of her hands funneling into his hair.

"So what you're saying is I'm basically the whole package?"

Kate's laughter tied him up inside; he wanted to be the only one to make her laugh in just that way. He'd never thought much about the way a woman laughed. But when Kate did, it was like she opened up and pulled him in, and he didn't mind being stuck there for good.

"Yes, Elliot Peters, you are definitely the whole package."

He swung her up into his arms and dropped with her onto the couch. "Back at you."

Kate's fingers tugged and pushed as she stitched one of the dresses, laughing at the Christmas movie they'd chosen. Elliot returned from the kitchen, put a glass of wine beside her, and took a drink of his beer before setting it down. He didn't know how she could watch the movie and work on the dress at the same time. Carefully, so he didn't bump her, he sat down on the corner of the couch. She looked at him, smiled, and stopped sewing to sip her wine.

"Thanks. Why are you looking at me like that?"

Elliot picked up his beer again, just so he had something to do with his hands so he didn't reach out and touch her while she was busy. The need to touch her felt like a living part of him.

"Like what?"

Setting her wine down, she went back to sewing. "Like you're not quite sure what to make of me."

"I was just thinking I should take you out. We're already sitting at home watching a movie like an old married couple, you with your sewing, and me with my feet up on the couch. Or they would be if you didn't have dresses everywhere," he said, gently teasing.

Kate laughed and set the sewing down on the ottoman in front of her. Clearing loose strings from her lap, she moved the scissors and pincushion, and then shifted closer to him.

With her thigh touching his, she reached out and took his hand. She traced her fingers over his palm and a shiver rode up his spine. Since when were his hands so goddamn sensitive? Since Kate.

She turned and smiled at him, tucking one knee up on the couch so they were facing each other.

"Can I tell you something?"

Elliot shifted his body and clasped her hand in his. "Anything. Always."

"I like dating," she said.

Elliot's heart stuttered. She meant him right? "Me."

Kate tilted her head. "What?"

"You like dating *me*," he said, hoping his voice wasn't shaky. He couldn't do the whole let's-see-other-people thing. He didn't want to push her or overwhelm her, but he didn't want to share either. He didn't know what the future would bring, but he wanted to give this relationship with her his—their—focus. They couldn't do that if they were dating other people. And he didn't want to date other people. Did she?

"Yes. Yes, I think dating you would be lovely, even though we technically haven't been out on a date."

Elliot took her other hand and tried to keep his voice even. He should have found a way to take her out. Maybe he could ask Lucy and Alex to babysit the girls. Just because they'd known each other forever didn't mean she wouldn't want all the little things she deserved. Candlelight dinners and actual dates.

"Elliot?"

He blinked. "What?"

Kate pulled one hand from his grip and touched his cheek, running her smooth palm over the rasp of a day's growth. "Why do you look upset?"

"I know I haven't taken you out yet. Even wanting this, it surprised the hell out of me how fast we happened. But I'm all in, Kate. I only want you. Do you really want *me* dating other women?"

Kate's eyes widened and froze. Then she blinked, several times. "What? Uh, no. No I do not. Is that where you thought I was going with this conversation?"

It was his turn to freeze. Sometimes shutting up really was the answer. "You weren't trying to tell me you want to date other guys?"

Kate went up on her knees and resettled herself so she was sitting in his lap. One of his hands went to her back and the other rested on her thighs. Her thin cotton pants couldn't contain the heat of her skin and he wished there was nothing between them. And that they weren't having this conversation.

Kate grinned. "I take it back. Maybe you're not so smart."

"Hey."

She rapped him on the chest. "You actually think that after sleeping with you last night, living in your house with you and your daughters and talking about being together, I'd be sitting here talking about dating other guys? Maybe you don't know me."

He winced. When she said it like that, his insecurity seemed stupid. But hell, his last relationship had no boundaries and not because he hadn't wanted them. The mildly wounded tone of Kate's voice made him ache.

"I know you." He ran his hand up her back and into her hair, tipping her head down so he could reach her mouth. "I know you. I'm sorry. I just don't really get where you're going with the whole 'I like dating' thing. I'll figure something out for the girls so we can go to a movie or dinner or something."

Kate's teeth grazed his bottom lip and he would have promised her anything at that moment. "It's not your turn to talk, Peters."

He laughed. "Sorry. You were saying?"

Pulling back a bit, she settled her hands on his shoulders and shifted in his lap, making it increasingly difficult to stay focused on her words. On her face. And not the feel of her against him.

"I was saying that I like dating. And I'd very much like you to take me out. For us to go out and do the whole dating thing. I have absolutely no interest in dating anyone other than you—just to set that record straight."

The muscles around his heart loosened. He nodded. "Noted. Happily."

She grinned, just one side of her mouth tipping up. "But, the old married couple thing sounds oddly appealing to me. *That's* what I was going to say. You date to get to know people, to test the waters and see if you have something that could last. I like this better. I like knowing who you are but not everything. There's enough I don't know to keep us going for a long time but enough that I do know that tonight feels… right. Like we don't have to go through all of the steps just to get here, where it feels good. Does that make any sense?"

He shifted, pulling her face to his. "It makes perfect sense. It should also be said, for the record, that I like it right here too. It feels as close to perfect as anything ever has or could."

He let his tongue trace her lips, let his hands roam and tighten against her hips. She sighed into his mouth, and he moved his hands back up to hold her face. He took his time kissing her; there were certain areas of the get-to-know-you phase he had no intention of skipping like finding out she liked how he nipped at her collarbone or how she shivered when he ran his fingertips up, over her ribs, across her breasts, and then back up into her hair.

"Elliot."

He liked hearing his name whispered from her lips and the way her breath caught as she inhaled.

Elliot stood clutching Kate in his arms, and she sighed again. "Jesus. You're romantic without even trying," she said, her arms looping around his neck.

Laughing, he walked them through the hushed quiet of the house. "I was going for expedient, but if you want to call it romance, I won't stop you."

They'd reached the threshold of both his bedroom door and the leash on his need for her when he heard the tiny voice.

"Why you carrying Kate, Daddy?"

Kate muffled a laugh and tapped his arm. He let her slide down his body, and the sensation was nearly painful. He turned, keeping Kate partially in front of him as he looked down and saw Beth holding her pillow. Her hair was everywhere, and she was still half-asleep.

"Sometimes big girls like to be carried, too," Kate said, shooting Elliot a wink.

Kate kneeled down in front of him so she was eye level with Beth, and the resulting view made it difficult for Elliot to separate being a dad from being a man. He took a couple of breaths and pulled himself together. He'd never lived with a woman other than Gina, but she was their mom so it had been normal to go to bed with her every night. He had no idea what to say to the girls about falling in love with their nanny, but he didn't want to sleep away from Kate.

"Daddy's a good carrier," Beth said, coming closer.

Kate scooped her up and Beth's head dropped to her shoulder. "So are you, Kate," she whispered. Elliot's heart squeezed like it was being flattened. They were so natural together.

"Thanks, sweetie. How come you're up?"

"It's Grace's turn for the doll, and I can't sleep without her," Beth said.

That damn doll. It was a piece of fucking fabric. Like Gina's sister couldn't have just gotten two?

"Can I sleep with you, Daddy?"

Kate turned, her eyes meeting Elliot's. The line between desire and responsibility played tug of war in his heart.

"Of course you can, baby." He pulled Beth into his own arms, his eyes on Kate's, hoping she could read the apology in them.

With a soft smile, Kate tipped her head to kiss Beth's cheek. Elliot held his breath as she went up on tiptoe and did the same to him.

"Sleep well," Kate said.

Before he could say anything else, not that he knew what to say, Kate walked down the hallway. He saw her turn into the girls' room first, likely to check on Grace. He stood there, holding Beth and rubbing her back as he watched. Sure enough, Kate stepped back into the hall, stopped when she saw him, and gave a small wave. Then she let herself into her own bedroom and shut the door.

"I'm sleepy, Daddy," Beth murmured.

He kissed her head and tucked her in beside him. Staring at the ceiling, he listened to the sound of Beth's deepening breaths. It didn't matter if he closed his eyes or not, Kate was all he could see. This was part of life with kids: interruptions, detours, and bumps. Kate was the first woman he'd ever looked forward to navigating those with. And the next time she was in his bed, or anywhere near him, he planned to tell her that.

Chapter Thirteen

Kate lugged bags of presents, both wrapped and unwrapped, into her parents' home. Instrumental Christmas music played softly but other than that, it was peacefully quiet, especially for the Aarons household. When the porch door slammed behind her, her mom appeared in the covered area, an apron wrapped around her full, curvy figure.

At sixty, their mom was still a looker. Both of her parents were attractive and charming. Quirky, with their own deeply set issues that Kate knew they still struggled with at times. But they gave and received love like it was life's currency and they were rich.

"There's my girl. Let me take some of that," Julie said, stepping onto the porch without a second thought.

Hard to believe only a couple years ago, it was a step Julie couldn't have taken. When she'd returned from Africa, Lucy had finally voiced the concern no one else would admit: their mom had become agoraphobic. Saying it out loud had not only made it real, but it had forced them all to face it, deal with it, and support Julie's recovery.

"Thanks. No peeking! I still have wrapping to do. You have the house to yourself?"

"I do. Char and Luke are working and your father took Carmen and Mia Christmas shopping."

Kate put the bags her mother didn't take onto the floor, tugged off her shoes and winter gear, and followed her mom into the house. The smell of gingerbread surrounded her, making her wistful and hungry at the same time. Setting the bags onto the table, she helped herself to one of the naked gingerbread men cooling on the pan.

"I haven't frosted them," Julie said, putting the other bags with the pile.

"They're better this way," Kate said, smiling around a large bite. "This is a treat. One-on-one time with you."

Kate loved her family, but quiet they were not. She rarely got time with just one of them, especially since she'd moved away. Missing people reminded her of getting hurt when she was little—until she realized the pain was there, it didn't bother her much. But once she noticed, there was little else she could focus on, which meant that regardless of what happened next, coming home had been the right thing to do.

Julie stepped closer and wrapped her arms around Kate. "A girl never gets too old to need her mom," Julie said into Kate's hair. "Thank God."

The words were a comfort, yet they sliced through her, poking at the nagging worry that she was entering a world of conflict by stepping into a "step-mom" role so quickly. She squeezed her mom back, trying to ignore the little voices piping up that said Kate could never be a substitute for a real mom. Regardless of how flighty Gina was, Beth and Grace loved their mom. Not that Kate wanted to change anything, she just wanted to find her own place.

"You okay?" Julie held her by the shoulders and looked her over with what always felt like a superhuman gaze.

Not much got past her mom. Kate knew her mom was as human as the rest of them, despite her mother's intuition. She was flawed and dented on the inside, but if anything, it only made her more genuine in her daughters' eyes. A real role model.

"I'm good." It was mostly true. Which was why it shocked her as much as her mother when she blurted out the rest. "I hated New York other than the internship. That part was perfect, the rest was not at all. All those things they tell you about the city? They're all true, but who really needs sushi at three a.m.? And I hated the subways. I never once felt like a local, and more often than not, I was irritated by the crowds and the noise. Not one barista ever learned my name at the Starbucks I went to every single day." She paused and caught her breath. "And I fell for a married man who I didn't know was married and I felt... just awful. Disgusted. I've never in my life ever thought of being *that* woman and the moment I realized I was, I walked away. But it's like it clings to me—knowing I was with another woman's husband. And I'm over it. I'm over him and New York, and what have I done? I've fallen right back down for someone else's man. I'm a disgusting human being."

She topped her rant off perfectly by bursting into tears. Her mom pulled her close again, her arms a vice gripping her like the strength of her hug could absorb all of the ache and the hurt, the uncertainty and the feeling of being misplaced.

"We need more than gingerbread for this," Julie muttered.

She walked away and Kate used the moment to take a few deep breaths.

Julie came back with a festive gift bag.

Kate groaned. "Mom. I love you, but I swear, herbal tea is not going to fix anything inside of me."

Julie laughed, set the bag on the counter, and got out two tumblers. "I both agree and disagree. But you're right, this situation calls for more than tea."

Julie lifted a tissue paper-covered bottle of whiskey out of the bag and held it up for Kate's inspection. She winked at her daughter and cracked the top. "Thanks to one of your father's colleagues, I've got something a bit stronger. Though I will make you some tea after. I have a new blend."

Of course she did. Her guru mother, who'd written over a dozen self-help books, had a cure for anything. What she didn't seem to understand was that *she* was the cure, not her remedies. It was Julie Aarons and her hard hugs, her quick wit, her no-strings-attached, no-holds-barred, fierce love.

"I'm sorry, Mom," Kate whispered as Julie passed her a glass with a very generous amount of scotch.

"What on earth for?"

"I feel like I've been all over the map. Metaphorically speaking," Kate added. Her sister Lucy had been all over the literal map before she'd finally come home to stay. Maybe it could work out for Kate too.

"All roads lead you where you're meant to be," Julie said, taking a sip of her drink.

"You really believe that?"

"With all my heart. It's why I'm standing here about to reprimand my youngest for several things and damn grateful I can do that."

Kate took a large gulp and steeled herself, knowing she deserved the lecture. Her parents had instilled better morals in her than the ones she had on display currently. Gina and Elliot weren't married but they would always be a family. Hadn't Kate just learned not to poke holes in the delicate structure of someone else's life? Goddamn Darby. Yet, here she was, diving in with her eyes open this time.

"Did you know he was married?"

Kate met her mother's gaze. "No. Absolutely not. The minute I found out, I walked away."

Julie nodded. "You use him to get anywhere you needed to go?"

Kate gasped. "No."

"Good." Julie nodded again. "You want to be here? Home? Or are you just running away? Not saying there's anything wrong with it if you are, because sometimes it's what needs to be done."

"I'm home because I want to be. I would be here either way. I miss you guys, I miss my family, I miss home, and I miss myself."

Julie's smile was a hug in itself. "You're right here, sweetheart. Have been all along. You don't get to be the person you're meant to become without some bumps in that proverbial road."

Kate sat down at the kitchen table and poked through the bag of toys for her nieces. "I guess."

Julie sat across from her and waited until Kate looked back up. "Not 'I guess.' It's true. This latest bump, Elliot?"

Kate could only nod.

"He's not anyone else's except those girls. As long as you can accept them, you're not doing anything wrong. Stop punishing yourself for following your heart and trusting in people."

Kate's tears resurfaced. "My small business loan got approved," she said. The bank had called as she was loading her car up with shopping bags an hour ago.

Julie grinned, jumped up out of her chair, and threw her arms around Kate's neck. "Congratulations! All roads, remember?"

Squeezing her mom's arms, she laughed. "Ever the optimist."

Julie sat back down and pushed her drink aside. "My darkest moments have sometimes led me to the brightest places. You know that. All three of you girls know that and were right here supporting me when I didn't think I could handle it."

"I love you, Mom. You're amazing." Julie waited for her to continue. Mother's intuition again, Kate supposed. "I'm not their mom."

"No. And you never will be. Doesn't mean you can't hold a special place in their lives. And in his."

Elliot seemed to want it that way and so did Kate. It was such a strange feeling to have all of her walls tumbling down around her, but feel like her feet were firmly planted on the ground. In the midst of the chaos, Kate felt like she was finally finding herself, pulling herself out of the rubble.

She sniffed, took another sip of scotch, and winced. "I need these wrapped. Wanna help?"

"I absolutely do," Julie said. "Take them into the living room. I'll put on the kettle for some tea."

Kate just laughed and did as she was told.

It was easier to wrap the gifts at her parents' house as she was leaving them there for Christmas Eve and Christmas morning. She and Elliot hadn't talked about either day yet. She knew he was off work thanks to Cam and Mick, two deputies without children who'd volunteered to cover the shifts. She wanted to see Beth and Grace's faces when they came out to see their stockings and gifts on Christmas morning. But she didn't want to miss Emma, Mia, or Carmen's faces either. Lucy and Alex would start their morning with Emma but be over immediately after as Luke and Char were staying at the Aarons' house through the holidays.

Julie had gently suggested that it wouldn't change much to add an extra three bodies to the sea of chaos. But Kate had no idea what Elliot envisioned for his girls. She'd missed him during the day. And the girls. They'd spent every day, practically every moment, together since she'd returned. Elliot had today off and had hinted that he and the girls had some secret shopping to do. Since Kate had plenty of her own, she'd left early in the day to get things done.

As she took the turn to his house, she thought about how to tell him her loan had been approved. Maybe tonight, in front of the fireplace and the Christmas tree. And while they were in the midst of celebrating—she knew he'd be thrilled for her—she'd ask him about spending Christmas with her family.

Maybe she should have texted and asked him about dinner. She could whip something up easily enough. She was thinking about how easy it was to slide into domesticity with him when she pulled up in front of his house. A strange car was in the driveway.

Thinking nothing of it, she grabbed the few purchases she hadn't wanted to leave at her parents' place and the doll she'd finally finished for the girls. She was all the way into the house, boots off, when she heard a voice. A voice she didn't know well enough to recognize because they'd only ever had brief conversations in passing.

Kate stepped into the kitchen to see Gina sitting at the table with two very excited little girls and Elliot. He was leaning against the counter, staring at them.

Her heart sank right down to her stomach like it was being yanked down by an anchor. She felt like she was standing in someone else's spot. They were a family and Kate was the nanny. A family friend. She must have made a strangled sound while standing in the doorway watching, a funny-looking doll clutched in one hand and the strap of her purse gripped tightly in the other.

"Kate," Elliot said.

Was it her imagination or did he say her name like he was giving thanks? Both girls shouted her name and came running. They were all about Kate for two seconds before they spotted the doll.

"Is that mine?" Beth asked.

"No. This one is mine," Grace said. They both looked up at Kate with identical expressions.

Kate's eyes moved back to Elliot. She couldn't read his face. She also couldn't breathe. Was it hot? The air felt thick. Gina stood and walked closer to Elliot. Kate's throat constricted.

Looking down at Beth and Grace, she worked up a smile. "Go get the other one, okay?"

They both ran to their room, and Gina gave her a small smile.

"Elliot said you were babysitting our girls. That's nice. Don't you have the day off though?"

Little razors slashed at Kate's heart. Had they been playing pretend for the past few days? *No. Elliot has made his feelings for you clear. More than that, he's made his feelings for Gina clear.*

"Gina. Jesus. That's not what I said. Kate come all the way in. I'm glad you're home," Elliot said, reaching out a hand for her.

Kate didn't take it but she came into the kitchen as the girls ran back with the doll they shared. Ignoring the ache in her chest and both the adults in the room, Kate knelt down, took the other doll, and hoped they were as good a match as she'd wanted. She put both dolls behind her back.

"Beth, you're older so you get to decide. Pick a hand and that'll be the doll you get," Kate said.

"That's not fair," Grace said, her lips curling into a pout.

"I know. Sometimes things aren't fair, sweetie. I have two older sisters. But there are perks to being the youngest sometimes, too."

Grace shrugged and looked at Beth. Her lips were also pursed, but in deep consternation.

Finally, she pointed to Kate's right arm. Handing that doll to Beth and the other to Grace, she held her breath. They inspected the dolls closely.

Finally Beth spoke. "Which one did you make?"

Air whooshed out of Kate's lungs. She laughed and pulled both the girls into a hug. "I forget and now it doesn't matter."

The girls thanked her, kissing her cheeks simultaneously. They went to play, and Kate stood in the kitchen, feeling like it was smaller than it had been the last time she was in it.

Elliot's eyes pleaded with hers but she didn't know what he was asking for. Gina's gaze was more of a glare.

"I, um…I'm actually going back to my parents' house. I just came to grab my stuff," Kate said. She hated lying but it wouldn't be a lie if that was where she ended up.

"There's no need for that. Gina is here for one night. She's leaving tomorrow," Elliot said.

"You said we'd talk," Gina said.

Elliot shot some fire of his own, directly toward Gina. She backed up a step. "We *did* talk. You forgot to listen. Why don't you go check on the girls? It's them you came to see."

He didn't wait for her to answer before turning to Kate, who stood like a statue, trying not to breathe. The air was tainted with Gina's scent. Elliot's. Her own. And one of those didn't belong. Elliot took her shoulders, digging his fingers into her skin, and held her gaze just as hard as he'd held Gina's, but with a softness that should have eased her mind.

"She just showed up. Said she wanted to talk about custody. My bet is she ran out of money and came home."

Home. Elliot's home and at one time, Gina's. Not Kate's. Pain pulsated through her like it was in her blood.

"You don't have to explain, Elliot. She's the mother of your daughters. There's no replacement for that. I just need to grab the dresses to take back to the rec center, and I'll be out of your hair." *And your home.*

Kate had a quick flashback of the first boy who'd broken her heart when she was sixteen. He'd ripped it to shreds and then lit fire to the tiny pieces. And still, when he'd called a few weeks later, she'd given him another chance. He tore her apart again, but she'd given him that chance because she'd loved him. She hadn't had children with him, and she'd still felt the pull to try again. How could Elliot not feel… something?

"I don't want you out of my hair. I want her out of my house. But she's here for the night because she told the girls that before I could stop her. I don't want to disappoint them, so I told her this is her chance to spend Christmas with them. Tonight. Tomorrow, she's gone."

His face was too close. Focusing on his words was difficult when she wanted to lean in, press herself against the strength of his body, and curl up into his arms where, for just a small piece of time, she'd felt like she belonged.

"I should go. So you guys can have your Christmas," Kate said. Her eyes dropped to his mouth.

His grip loosened but the intensity of his voice did not. "You don't need to go. I don't want you to go."

Kate's throat was tight, but she pushed the words through. "I need to take the dresses to Cole. I promised. Maybe Gina wants to stick around for the play on Christmas Eve."

She could be mature. It might kill her, or at the very least, make her gag, but she could do it. And if she really wanted something with Elliot, she'd need to be. She'd have to learn to accept this part of his life. But first, she needed to give him the space to make sure he wasn't saying goodbye to a chapter he wasn't ready to finish. She couldn't do that if she stayed here tonight, or any night when Gina was there. "I…uh. I'll be here tomorrow to watch the girls but when you get home, I'm going to stay with Lucy and Alex. I can bunk on their couch."

"Kate," he said. The word was a harsh whisper, filled with sadness and disappointment.

One of the girls was yelling in the other room about something being hers. The sound intensified, and Elliot winced.

"Goddammit. I'll be right back. She can't handle them for five fucking minutes."

He stalked away from her, and Kate finally filled her lungs and let out a breath. Walking to her room, Kate grabbed a few things for the night and then went to grab the dresses from the living room. Gina stood at the window looking out but turned when Kate entered.

"Those are pretty," she said.

"Thanks," Kate said, scooping them up in her arms, trying not to lose purchase of the bag over her shoulder.

"It's not easy, you know," Gina said.

Kate held the woman's gaze, noticing how tired she looked. The creases around her eyes and the sallow look of her skin made her seem older than she was.

"What's that?"

"Being a mom. I didn't ask for this. I'm trying," Gina said.

Fury melted away Kate's lingering guilt. "Are you?"

Gina's eyes widened. "Excuse me?"

"It doesn't matter what you asked for, Gina. You have two beautiful little girls with an amazing man who would do anything for them. Or you for that matter. Life isn't all about you anymore. So if what you've given is the best you have, dig deeper and find more. Do more. Try harder. They deserve it."

She didn't wait; she turned and headed for the door. Elliot caught her just as she was about to step onto the porch.

"Wait," he said.

She turned, unsure how long she could hold off the tears. Looking up at him, she did as he asked. He didn't say anything. He looked at her as if she could give him the answers they needed, but she didn't have any.

"I have to go," Kate said. "I'm sorry. It feels too weird to stay when she's here. The girls need time with their mom for Christmas. And maybe you need some sort of…I don't know, closure. I need you to be sure. I know you said you are. I'm not doubting your feelings for me, but she's the mother of your kids. There have to be feelings there too."

He started to speak but Kate left. She couldn't listen, not now. Not when the tears were already starting to leak because no matter what he chose, his life would always be inextricably tied to the woman in his house. Kate wasn't sure how to wrap her head around that when she'd only just realized she was in love with all three of them: Elliot and his daughters.

Growing up, she'd imagined that one day she'd have a husband and a family. But it hadn't looked like this in her head. She hadn't shared their children with another woman. How did people do this and know, without a doubt, that the other person was completely theirs? How could Elliot ever be as sure about her as she was about him?

Upon pulling out of his driveway, she headed for the rec center, ignoring the tears dampening her cheeks. With a degree in social work, Kate knew that in every instance possible, families were kept together because family mattered. Not step-moms or girlfriends or nannies. Families. Linked and bound in a way Kate could never be with the girls.

Chapter Fourteen

Elliot tucked Beth in for the third time. The first time she'd needed water. The second, she'd had a bad dream (even though she hadn't fallen asleep), and this time, she'd needed the bathroom (thanks to the water).

"Stay in bed this time, okay?"

Beth snuggled in, yawning. "When will Kate be home?"

"Tomorrow. I love you."

Grace snored softly. Elliot leaned over to kiss her temple before giving Beth one more kiss.

"I love you, too. Are we going to spend Christmas with Kate, Daddy?"

Elliot froze, looking down at her. "Do you want to?"

Beth's eyelids were drooping but she nodded. "Yes. I think she wants a puppy, too."

Chuckling, Elliot walked to the door. "Goodnight, Beth."

"I'm not joking, Daddy. I asked Santa to get one for her and you and one for me and Gracie to share."

"That's a lot of puppies."

"Kate said in her house, her mom says the more, the married."

Another laugh escaped. He could correct the expression another time. For now, he just found it utterly adorable. "Goodnight, Beth."

"Night, Daddy."

The look on Kate's face was burned into Elliot's brain. She'd told him to find "closure" and be sure. She'd left before he could tell her what he and Gina had was over before it began. And as to being sure? He only needed time to show Kate exactly how sure he was—a lifetime should work. Something he'd never wanted, not for one second, with any other woman.

But she was right about one thing, he needed to sort Gina out because if his life was going to involve another woman in the way he wanted it to, there had to be some boundaries and he intended to set them.

Gina was drinking a beer when he came into the living room. She hadn't brought the girls gifts. She'd shown up and asked for a place to stay for the night because things hadn't worked out with her sister. Big surprise. He'd given her eight years to figure out what she wanted and get her shit together. But she hadn't. Time to stop playing nice and start doing what was best for the girls.

He took a seat across from her. "I'm going to sue you for full custody. You'll need a lawyer."

Gina choked on her beer. She sat forward, coughing and sputtering, until her eyes watered. Elliot maintained a grim look, determined not to cave. At one time, he'd been willing to give things between them a real shot for the girls' sake. He could see now, looking at her, that he'd never feel for her what he felt for Kate. Who knew why? His life would be a hell of a lot easier if he could be head over heels in love with the mother of his children. But he wasn't and he never had been, so he needed to help her move forward so she could be part of their lives in the next best way.

"You son of a bitch. You know I can't afford a lawyer," Gina said, wiping her mouth.

"Not my problem. I'm done playing. You show up when you want, do what you want. You never put them first."

"It hasn't exactly been easy for me," she said.

"That's what you don't get," he said, trying to keep his voice low. "It's not about *you*. It's about them."

"We could try again. We could be a family. I'll be better," Gina said, scooting forward.

Elliot shifted back in his chair. "I don't want that. Not with you."

Gina took another long swallow of her beer and then sneered at him. "But you want it with Kate?"

"It's not about her either. We were never a good fit. You know that as well as I do. But we have two little girls, and I want them to grow up knowing their mom. You need to figure out your life, get a job, pull yourself together. Get a goddamn apartment and put down some roots. Hell, maybe try counseling."

She stood and stalked to the window. The snow had started about an hour ago, and the flakes were the size of quarters.

"God. You're so self-righteous. Everything is so easy for you so you don't get it. I am trying, and I said I'd do better. We don't need lawyers. They can stay with you," she said.

He gave a short laugh. "It's not enough. You've said all of this before. Many times. I want signed documents. I'll be going to a lawyer right after the holidays. You can contest it if you want but you won't win, even if you can afford to get a lawyer."

She stared at him, leaning against the wall like she'd suddenly gone weary. "You know I can't, so fine. You take them. I'll sign whatever papers I have to. I just want to be able to see them. I know I'm not the best at this, but I do love them."

Elliot stood, his heart in his throat. "Good. Then you'll know I only want what is in their best interests when I tell you that I'll be asking the judge for supervised visitation only until you've firmly established yourself. That means a job and a place to live, here in Angel's Lake or somewhere close enough that they can visit you for an afternoon."

Her eyes went impossibly dark, glazing over with fury. "Fuck you, Elliot. You're not in charge of me."

He shook his head. "Nope. But you're not taking them across any state line ever again. You want to see them, you come here. Get a job, get a place in town, prove you can be a responsible adult, and you can have them more often. But until you pull yourself together, for real this time, we're done. You can stay tonight. Tomorrow I want you gone. The next time I see you, it'll be in a court."

She didn't cry. Gina wouldn't. One of the things that had attracted him to her was her tough exterior. She'd been carefree and vibrant when they'd met so long ago. He'd liked that since he'd always felt like he was the opposite. He'd enjoyed indulging her and hadn't minded that she'd been a little self-involved. She was no-strings-attached and that had suited him. Until they'd had the girls. Then everything had shifted. His entire world had adjusted and zoomed into focus, and he'd waited too long hoping that Gina would adjust and focus too.

"You can't do this," she said.

Elliot shook his head. "I have to. One of us has to make the right decisions for them. I'm tired of waiting for it to be you."

She walked up to him and put her hands on his chest, lowering her lashes in a way he knew she thought was seductive. "What would it take for us to try again? What would I have to do to make you want me? Love me?"

Elliot gripped her shoulders and set her back from him. "You'd have to be Kate. I'm sorry if that hurts you. She has nothing to do with why I need you to step up and be better for Beth and Grace, but if you're asking what it would take for me to love you the way a man is supposed to love a woman he wants to spend the rest of his life with? Then you'd have to be Kate Aarons."

He didn't mean to cause her pain, but he realized, watching her absorb the truth, that he'd inadvertently hurt her anyway…all these years of never just laying it out. They'd been over before they had the girls but Gina had always thought the door was open because he'd let her see it that way. He shouldn't have and he'd have to live with knowing he could have been more careful with her feelings.

She started to go but he took her arm. She looked up at him.

"I want you to sort yourself out, Gina. I'll help if I can. I'll pay for counselling if you want it. If you make an effort, a real effort to prove you want the girls to be a part of your life and that you'll put them first, I'll help. I'll get papers drawn up for custody. If you sign them, I won't go through the courts. You won't have to worry about paying for a lawyer or fees. You can just worry about figuring out your life."

Gina pulled her arm from his hand and snapped at him, "And what do I get out of that?"

Jesus. She just didn't get it. "A hell of a lot more than you'll get without it. Your choice."

This time, he walked away. He wanted this night over so he could have Kate home and he could tell her how sure he really was. So he and his girls could spend what he hoped would be the first of many Christmases with Kate and her family.

Maybe he would take a look at puppies, just in case Beth was right. Couldn't hurt, could it?

Elliot stood outside of Alex and Lucy's house at five a.m. the next morning. Gina and the girls were still sleeping. He had to work at six and then he'd be off for a few days, but he couldn't go the whole day without Kate. He just didn't know how to see her without waking her family. He had his hands on his hips and was studying the door when it opened.

Kate was pulling a knit cap over her wild bed head. She froze midstep as she let out a squeal then quickly slapped a hand over her mouth. Elliot took the stairs of the porch two at a time, barely reaching her when Alex came flying to the door.

"Kate? What's wrong? What the hell, Elliot?" Alex glared, putting a protective hand on Kate's shoulder.

She leaned into him with such casual ease, it made Elliot's heart cramp. "Sorry. I didn't mean to scream. He startled me. I'm fine," she said.

"I didn't mean to scare you," Elliot said.

"What are you doing lurking around my house at five a.m.? You're on shift at six," Alex said.

Even wearing checkered pajama bottoms and a long-sleeve pajama top, Alex exuded authority.

"I know that. I had to see Kate. I'm sorry."

Alex looked back and forth between them with eyes that Elliot knew picked up on everything. He kissed Kate on the crown of her head. "Let me know if you want me to kick his ass."

Kate laughed. "I'm good. Go get your coffee."

"See you when I get in at seven, Peters," Alex said, shutting the door.

Kate stood in front of him, her face peeking out of the space between her cap and her jacket collar.

"Hey," he said.

"Hi. It's kind of early. Were you worried I wouldn't show up?"

"Yes. But not like you mean," he said.

He'd gone over the words a dozen times last night but now they were bouncing around inside of him like rubber balls.

She rubbed her hands together. "It's pretty cold out here. Is everything okay?"

Elliot took her hands between his own gloved ones, and warmed them. "I hope so. I had this all planned out. I knew what I was going to say, but the minute I look at you, I forget everything except how much I want you."

Her lips pursed. "That's a good thing to say."

"I don't need any closure. Gina and I were over before we began. Without the girls, we never would have lasted. I tried because of them, but I've always known it wasn't her. That hasn't ever bothered me because I just want what's best for the girls. But what scares me is figuring out that it's *you,* knowing it'll be you for the rest of my life whether you want me or not. I wondered why I couldn't make it work with her—besides the obvious. I thought maybe I should try harder and expect less. But it wasn't just her. I mean, I've dated other women since her." He let go of her hands, took his gloves off, and passed them to her. She tugged them on, her mouth slightly open as she watched him carefully.

"It wasn't right with any of them so I thought maybe I'm just not going to have *that*. Whatever that was. To be honest, I didn't really know what it was before you. I've seen it. I see it in the way Alex looks at Lucy and Luke looks at Char. Hell, even the way your dad looks at your mom. I'd seen it, but I'd never felt it. And that was okay because I had the girls. I was happy. Content. But then you came back and we…I don't even know. All the moments where I'd felt something for you in passing kind of magnified when I saw you get out of the cab. And then we kissed and I knew. I'm sure in a way I've never been sure about anything else in my life. You're it for me. I love you, Kate. I know that asking you to be part of my life means asking you to be an insta-mom. I don't know how you feel about that. It means date nights will probably be on the couch at home, unless your family wants to babysit. And it means Gina. For a good, long time."

He ran out of words and cursed himself silently for not ending on a better note. Why hadn't he *ended* with "I love you" rather than ending with what sounded like a life sentence.

The blue of her eyes sparkled in the bright, cool morning. They were like jewels, shimmering with unshed tears.

"Are you done?"

His heart tumbled, crashing into his stomach. He nodded. He shouldn't have let her walk out last night. What the hell had he been thinking?

Kate walked over to the railing and leaned against it. Her puffy jacket rustled against the cold wood. Elliot stayed still, hoping that her words wouldn't stab holes in his heart that would never close. He knew she needed a turn to talk but really, he just wanted to grab her and yank her close, kiss her until some of the pressure weighing on his chest eased up.

"I feel like I've been jumping around for a couple of years, bouncing from one thing to another and that's not who I am. Lucy convinced me to follow my heart when I went to New York. So I did and it felt good. But not…right. So even though I was worried about disappointing her, I followed my heart again and came home. That felt even better because I'm back where I want to be and I'm going to be able to open my own place where I can sell my designs."

"I'm really happy you get to do that here in Angel's Lake. You belong here," he said. He could be proud of her and happy for her, even if it meant having to see her every day but not getting to be with her.

"I think so too. When I came back, it felt…right. But not good. Do you know what I mean?"

The cold was beginning to numb his body parts. "Not really."

She pushed off the railing and now she took his hands in hers, his gloves dwarfing her fingers.

"When you kissed me, it felt right and good and exactly like I'd always imagined it would."

His heart twitched in his stomach, stirring with hope at her words. "Imagined what would?"

She smiled. "*It. That.* The feeling of being with someone and knowing they are exactly the right person for you. That they're the reason nothing else fit. And how lucky am I that I not only get to have my dream of designing clothes, but I get to do that in the only place that's ever been home, with a man that I admire and respect? And love."

His heart danced its way back to his chest. "Love?"

Kate wound her hands around his waist, pulling them as close as they could be with two winter jackets between them. "Yes. I always thought I'd meet a man, fall in love, and have a family. I've always wanted that. I didn't know I'd meet a man, become his friend, and fall in love with him and his ready-made family. But I did. I love you. I love Beth and Grace, and I want this. I don't know how this works and I'm scared. More scared than I was heading off to a giant city all by myself at twenty-two. More scared than I was of coming home and disappointing my family. But it feels good and it feels right. So I'm sure too."

"Thank, God. I'm so sorry I let you leave last night. I should have begged you to stay. Don't leave again. I don't want to spend another night away from you."

Kate went up on her tiptoes, touching her nose to his. "That's handy because I really don't want to spend another night away from you knowing Gina's with you instead."

"She's not you. No one could ever be you," he said.

Unable to wait any longer, he kissed her and kept kissing her until he forgot how damn cold it was, forgot that he had to get to work, forgot they were standing on her sister's porch next door to her parents' house. Forgot everything but Kate.

Until the door flew open again and Alex charged through. "Elliot. There's been an accident. Gina and the girls. They're on route to the hospital."

Chapter Fifteen

In his life, Elliot had never known fear that settled so deep into his skin, into his bloodstream, and consumed him to the point of pain. Alex drove with the sirens on. Kate sat in the back of Alex's cruiser as they whipped toward the hospital. No one spoke and the silence was deafening. He couldn't breathe.

Kate's hand came to rest on his shoulder. She squeezed and he covered her fingers with his. She was still wearing his gloves. In seconds, his life had gone from absolute happiness to extreme terror.

"Almost there," Alex said, his voice strong and solid like the foundation of the earth.

They're okay. They're okay. They're going to be okay.

The snow-slicked roads didn't help and more than once, he felt Kate's fingers clench on his shoulder. But she didn't say a word.

When the car pulled up to the emergency entrance, Elliot shot out of the car and flew through the automatic doors before Alex had shifted into park.

Cam, one of the other deputies, was talking with a nurse. He saw Elliot and came to him, his face a mask of calm, making Elliot fear the worst.

"They're okay. They're all okay," Cam said.

Alex and Kate must have been directly behind him because he heard Alex speak at the same time he felt Kate's arms come around him from the side.

"What happened?" Alex asked.

"I need to see them. Now," Elliot said.

He pulled away from Kate, but she gripped his hand as Cam spoke.

"She crashed into a telephone pole. The roads are slick; she was going too fast," Cam said.

The deputy was looking at Alex but Elliot heard something in his tone that made anger douse his fear.

"What else?" Elliot demanded. Kate squeezed harder.

Cam looked at Alex, then back at Elliot, and cleared his throat. "She had bags packed for Beth and Gracie. I think she was headed out of town."

Like the terror had, anger cloaked him, covering him like another layer of skin. "That fucking bitch. She'll never see them again. I'll make sure—"

Kate stood in front of him, grabbed his face between her hands, and stopped his words. Tears trailed over her cheeks. He could barely see them or her through the haze. He felt like he was outside of himself.

"They're okay. That's all that matters," she said.

She wrapped her arms around him and even though he had fifty pounds on her at least, she clutched so hard he lost his breath. When it whooshed out, so did some of the haze. He held on, scared to let go. Scared for the next part.

"I need to see the girls," Elliot said into her hair, his voice cracking.

"I'll get the doc," Cam said.

Alex put a hand on Elliot's back while Kate kept her body glued to his.

"Just focus on the girls. We'll deal with the rest later," Alex said.

A white-haired doctor came up to where they stood huddled in the entry of the waiting room. Kate stepped back but kept hold of his hand.

"Mr. Peters?"

Elliot reached out a hand. "Officer Peters. Angel's Lake Police Department. I need to see my daughters, Beth and Grace Peters."

He needed all the leverage he could get. If being a cop got him in one second sooner, he'd take it.

"Both of your daughters are fine. They were wearing their seatbelts, unlike the driver," the doctor said. He looked down at the chart in his hand. "Beth fractured her left forearm. We've put a cast on it. Grace has minor contusions on her face from broken glass. She needed four stitches on one arm but is otherwise fine."

Elliot's eyes burned. His babies, hurt. Okay, but definitely hurt. Because he'd done what anyone should be able to do: he'd left them with their mother.

"What about Gina, the driver?" Kate asked.

Elliot looked down at her, amazed that she had the compassion to ask. He was so goddamn mad he wondered if he'd ever feel compassion again.

The doctor looked at the chart again, flipped a page. "As I said, she wasn't wearing her seatbelt, but she's lucky she wasn't hurt worse. She has three broken ribs, a broken collarbone, and a concussion. We'll need her to stay tonight at least."

"You can keep her as long as you want. I want to see my daughters.

Now."

The doctor nodded and Elliot immediately followed when he started walking toward the swinging doors. "That's fine. I'll sign their discharge papers. You can go back with the deputy. He's already been to see them."

Kate stood still and Elliot stopped. "Come. Please."

She came to his side immediately and walked through the swinging doors with him. The girls were in a bed together, sitting up and holding hands. Grace started to cry the second she saw him. He and Kate both rushed forward and Elliot carefully wrapped his arms around them.

"You're okay. You guys are going to be okay. I love you both so much," Elliot said.

Tears stung, and he couldn't stop them any more than he could stop his heart from vibrating in his chest. He wanted to pull them inside of his body and promise them they'd never be hurt again. That he'd do a better job protecting them.

"Daddy, I got a cast," Beth said.

Her eyes showed she'd been crying, but she wasn't now. Grace hiccupped and Kate grabbed some Kleenex.

"I got stitches," Grace said, hiccupping again.

"You two are so brave," Kate said, dabbing at Grace's tears.

"Mommy said we had to go somewhere else. She wouldn't say where. We told her we couldn't because it was Christmas and we didn't want to, but she said it was just for a little while. Is Mommy okay?" Beth said.

Kate ran a hand down Beth's hair, kissed her cheek. "Your mom is going to be fine, sweetie."

Elliot unclenched his jaw, grateful that Kate still had the composure to say the right words. They weren't the ones that popped into his head.

Alex walked into the small curtained area. Cam must have gone back out to the waiting room, but Elliot hadn't seen him go.

"There's my favorite twins," Alex said. He handed them each a stuffed bear, one with a purple shirt and one with a green shirt.

"Hi, Officer Whitman. We got to drive in an ambulance," Beth said.

"What do you say Beth?" Elliot asked.

"Thank you," Beth said, squeezing the bear.

"Thank you," Grace said. She sniffed again and curled into Elliot. He boosted her up into his arms.

"You're welcome. You girls okay?" Alex asked.

"We're okay," Beth said.

"I'm hungry," Grace replied.

Alex laughed. "I bet your dad and Kate will take you out for breakfast. You can probably milk this pretty good. Get out of chores, get some extra treats."

Elliot chuckled and the rock in his chest dislodged. He could breathe again. They were okay.

"Thanks," Elliot said, managing a grin at Alex.

"Can we get a puppy?" Beth asked.

Kate laughed, lifting Beth down from the bed gently. "Good try, cutie."

"Uh, I'm supposed to be at work," Elliot said, just realizing it.

Alex's eyes narrowed and his lips tilted down. "And I expect you to be there right now? Jesus, Peters. I told you I don't want to have to kick your…" he started then looked at the girls, "butt."

Both girls giggled.

Alex shook his head and kissed Kate's cheek. "I'll see you guys on Christmas Eve, okay? Lucy thought it would be a good idea to host dinner at our house." He looked at Elliot again and pointed at him.

"You have some vacation time stored up. I don't want to see you until the first of the year."

Firming his lips to fight back emotions he didn't want to express, Elliot nodded. "Thanks."

Alex clapped him on the shoulder. "I'll take care of Gina's paperwork. Get your girls settled. All of them."

Alex walked to the nurse's station and Elliot looked down and saw Kate's hand grasping Beth's. Grace's arms squeezed his neck.

"Let's go. We'll get something to eat," Elliot said.

Kate hesitated. "Grace, can you walk, honey?"

Grace lifted her head from Elliot's shoulder and murmured, "Yes."

Kate rubbed a hand over her back and locked eyes on Elliot. "I'll get them in the car. Alex sent Cam for mine. He'll catch a ride back to the station with Alex. Go make sure Gina's okay."

"Kate."

"Elliot."

He didn't want to. He was afraid he'd say something he couldn't take back. But Kate was looking at him, believing he could go to the woman who'd put him through hell like it was a playground he enjoyed, put her own needs before that of their girls, and still be the bigger person. He wanted to be the man Kate saw. He nodded and set Grace on the floor.

When they walked back through the swinging doors, he turned to ask the nurses where Gina was and saw Alex watching him. He pointed to a curtain in the other corner of the large room.

Elliot opened the curtain, certain his fury would come back like an avalanche. Monitors beeped quietly. Gina's face was bruised. Part of her scalp was shaved where they'd put the stitches. Her eyes, dark and swelling, fluttered open, filling with tears.

"I'm so sorry," she whispered. Her voice cracked, mirroring the ache in his heart.

Elliot went to her side and without even thinking about it, took her hand.

She sniffed then winced. "I don't want to be this person. I'm so sorry," Gina said, tears pouring down her face.

Elliot grabbed a tissue and much like Kate had for Grace, dabbed at Gina's cheeks.

"You need help. I don't know what you need or how to help you myself, but something has to change," he said.

She nodded as she took the Kleenex from him and wiped at her eyes. Tears kept coming, and the pain in Elliot's chest receded, just enough to keep his voice gentle.

"You're better than this, Gina. Maybe you should speak to a counsellor or the doctor. I don't know, but you can't keep going with this self-destructive behavior. You need to build a life. One that includes our girls and keeping them safe."

Gina pulled her lip between her teeth and stared at the tissue in her hand. "I know. You've never given up on me."

Elliot's stomach cramped. He felt like he had. "You're their mom. They need their mom."

Her eyes met his and more tears flowed. Elliot didn't know what to do with them; he'd never seen her cry. Gently, he leaned his hip on the bed and passed her the tissue.

Gina's voice was small. "They'll have Kate."

Fighting his own emotions and the lump that reappeared in his throat, he nodded. "Yeah. They will. I love her, Gina. I want to be with her, so they'll have her and she'll be good to them. She'll love them. But they still need their mom."

Gina nodded as she took the tissue from Elliot's hand. "I don't know what to do," she whispered.

Elliot leaned over and kissed her forehead. "Get better. Get settled. Cal's always looking for waitresses at the diner. It's a start. I'll help you, but you have to work for it. It's not going to be easy."

Gina winced, and Elliot stood straight. "I know. I'm scared. But the thought of them being hurt, more than I've already hurt them, terrifies me."

Finally, something was getting through to her. "Talk to Cal. I'll give him a call." Elliot said. He could do that for her. She'd given him the girls.

He started to go before Gina said his name.

All of the tears were gone. "Why would you help me after everything I've done?"

He thought for a minute and then decided to give her the truth. "I'd do anything for them. I'm hoping this gives them their mom back."

She nodded, and Elliot left. He took a few deep breaths before he walked out of the hospital and pulled himself together. Or, together enough to get through breakfast. There was nothing he wanted more than to be home with all of his girls.

Chapter Sixteen

The panic of the last few days had faded, but Kate still felt wound up. Worry hovered inside her as she and Elliot pampered the girls and then maximized their alone time when both of them fell asleep. But even when he'd made love to her the last two nights, insisting she stay beside him, telling her how far he'd fallen, the nerves wouldn't settle. She had to keep reminding herself and reminding him that everything was okay.

"I hope you guys are ready for this," she said as the girls and Elliot stomped the snow off of their boots on Lucy and Alex's porch.

Elliot laughed and ran a hand down her hair, then leaned in and kissed her cheek. "We've hung out with your family, Kate." He pushed open the door without even knocking, and music and voices tumbled out as the girls ran in.

"It might be too much excitement for them after everything. Maybe we should have stayed home and just kept tonight quiet. Tomorrow will be chaotic too," Kate said.

Elliot framed her face with his hands. "They're okay. They want to be here."

Even though she believed him—could see in his eyes that he meant it—her stomach continued to tumble. This was big. She'd never even brought a date to a family event and here she was bringing a man she'd unexpectedly fallen in love with and his two children. Kate looked past him, knowing they had only seconds before someone in her family descended.

"Do you?" she asked. "Want to be here? It's a lot. They're a lot. We've jumped in, head, feet, whole body first."

Elliot rested his forehead against hers and she closed her eyes, breathing him in. "Kate. I want to be wherever you are. And for the record, I like your head, your feet, and your whole body. A lot."

Gripping his wrists, she opened her eyes and beamed up at him. His words went a long way toward loosening the pressure in her chest.

"Okay. But don't say I didn't warn you."

They managed to get into the house, hang their jackets, and make it to the kitchen before they were bombarded by her mother, who hugged Elliot tightly.

"We're so glad everyone is okay and that you're joining us for Christmas," Julie said.

Releasing her, Elliot smiled. "Thank you for making my girls and I feel so welcome."

Julie winked at him. "Back at you with my girl."

Then she hugged Kate and ushered them farther into the fray. Luke and Char were at the long, wide, gorgeously restored farm table, setting up Monopoly with Grace, Beth, and Carmen choosing their pawns. The dining room and kitchen were one large room, but the living room was through an arch. In it, Kate's dad was settled on the floor, back against one of the couches, amusing Emma and Mia. They were belly laughing in a way that made the rest of Kate's nerves fade away.

Mark stood. "There's my girl. Elliot," he said, shaking Elliot's hand and clapping him on the back. "Glad your girls are okay, son. Gina doing alright?"

"Yes, sir," Elliot said.

Kate glanced at him, confused by the stilted tone in Elliot's voice. She hugged her dad, hard, comforted by the scent of his cologne. He kissed the top of her head.

"I'm going to go help Alex and your mother with dinner. You okay to keep an eye on these two?" Mark asked, releasing her.

"I thought Lucy was making dinner," Kate said.

Lucy came down the stairs, her hair bundled on top of her head. "I am. Sort of. I just had to change. There was a potato mishap," she said, coming to Elliot and Kate.

Hopefully Elliot wasn't put off by her family of huggers. He didn't seem to mind when Lucy gave him one. "Glad the girls are okay. And Gina too."

"Thanks Luce. Can we help with anything?" Elliot asked, his tone even again.

"Just what Dad said. watch these two munchkins while we finish up in the kitchen," Lucy said.

Lucy tugged on a lock of Kate's hair. "It turns out I'm more of a sous chef," Lucy said.

Kate laughed. "Not surprising."

"Hey!" Lucy said, giving her a mock pout.

"You have many other talents, honey," Mark said, throwing one arm around Lucy's shoulder.

"Thanks, Dad."

Kate was still smiling as she sat on the floor with Emma and Mia. Emma picked up a book and brought it to Kate, but wouldn't hand it over.

She glanced at Elliot, who sat beside her on the floor. "You okay?"

He stacked some blocks on top of each other, waited until Mia was watching, and then tipped them over, making her laugh. "Yeah. Just…" He stopped and shrugged.

"Just what?"

Elliot stacked the blocks again. "I've been around your family lots. Just not after I've slept with and fallen in love with their youngest daughter," he whispered.

Kate laughed. "I think they'll still like you," she said.

"Let's hope so, seeing as I don't plan on putting a stop to either," he said.

By the time dinner was eaten, games were played, and they'd each opened a present, Kate was exhausted. She'd worried about the girls but they clearly had untapped reserves of energy. Luke and Char were packing up to go home, and Kate was about to suggest she and Elliot do the same when she caught sight of Lucy and Alex whispering to each other. His hand was on her hip and hers was on his chest. Alex swept a hand down Lucy's hair and kissed her forehead. It made Kate's stomach dip with happiness. She had that, too.

She looked at Elliot, who was tracing circles on her hand with his thumb. "We should go home," she whispered. Home. That word now held more meaning than she ever could have imagined.

"I think you have something to share before we do," he whispered back. His happiness and pride when she'd told him about the loan still set butterflies loose in her stomach.

"Now?"

"What better gift for you and everyone that loves you than knowing your future, the future you want, is right here where they are?"

He gave her hand an affectionate squeeze. Their day had been so busy with the Christmas play earlier that she'd barely had time to think. The girls had been adorable, and Kate had received a dizzying number of compliments on her designs. She had no doubt she'd be getting some custom orders and that grad season was going to keep her busy.

She stood up. "We have to get going, but I wanted to tell everyone something before we leave," Kate said.

It took a moment for everyone to quiet down and then they were all looking at her, waiting, ready for whatever she said. A wave of bliss stole her breath. Everyone she loved and needed was right here. She was truly going to have it all.

"We already know you have a crush on Elliot," Lucy said.

Kate glared at her but Julie spoke first. "Lucy, don't bug your sister."

Lucy stuck her tongue out, making both Kate and Char laugh, and Elliot nudged her foot.

"I got approved for a small business loan, and I've found a shop. I'm officially going to be opening my own dress boutique in Angel's Lake."

Everyone squealed in delight, rushing her all at once, including the kids, who hadn't really been paying attention but were happy to take part in the excitement. Kate wondered if there was a world record for the most hugs given in a day. If so, whatever the number, her family topped it.

In the quiet of the car, Elliot held Kate's hand. The girls were nearly asleep in the back seat, and Elliot and Kate had to each carry one of them into the house. They curled into their beds after being peeled out of their matching coats and were sleeping before Kate and Elliot left the room.

"I'm going to put on some pajamas. You want to watch a movie?" Kate asked.

Elliot kissed her, light and quick. "Sure. I'll put one on, grab some wine, and then we can fill stockings."

Kate laughed. "That sounds like code for something," she said.

Elliot gave her another kiss, this one noisy and playful. "That's after."

Kate took her time getting ready for bed, removing her make-up, and brushing out her hair. When she came into the living room, the lights were low, a movie was cued up, and two glasses of wine sat on the coffee table. But no Elliot. She heard a door and then he came into the living room with a sheepish expression.

"What are you doing?"

He walked to her, pulling her into his arms. "I'll tell you in a minute. Let's sit down first."

She sat, intrigued, but felt some of the tension seep back into her shoulders. He turned her so they were facing, pulled her as close as she could get without sitting on his lap, then passed her a glass of wine.

She sipped, watching him as he did the same.

"I'm proud of you. I think you're amazing and I want you to know that I'll do everything I can to support your dream."

She melted a little inside. "Thank you." Reaching out, she pressed her palm to his cheek. "That was a lovely thing to say."

"I mean it. I want our life together to be about compromise. I'll give you everything I have and never take you for granted." He laughed roughly. "I'll mess up. But I promise to buy flowers."

Kate laughed, setting her wine down, and scooted closer. "I'd rather have chocolate than flowers. What should I get you when *I* mess up?"

His eyes twinkled. "Guys are pretty easy."

She watched his gaze shift, become more serious. "How do you feel about kids?"

Elliot put his glass next to hers and took her hands, staring at them. When his gaze met hers, the emotion in them stopped Kate's breath, making it back up into her lungs.

"I love Grace and Beth, but I'm not looking to be their mom. I won't try to take Gina's place. Do you think all of this is too soon? Too fast? Too much?"

Elliot shook his head. "They love you back. They don't want you to leave. But that's not exactly what I meant."

Kate was letting the glow of his words warm her when she realized what he *did* mean. "Do you...do you want more kids?"

Now he tugged her hands, pulling her forward so she was nestled between his legs. "I didn't think so. In fact, I was sure I didn't. Until you. But I want that with you."

Kate's heart pounded against her rib cage rapidly, like it was punching its way out. "You do?"

"I do. I'm not usually big on fate or kismet or whatever you want to call it. But I feel like all of the things that have happened led us here. I've wanted to ask you out for years but the timing was never right. But no other time would have been right for either of us. We wouldn't be who we are right this minute without all of the things that brought us here."

Kate bit the inside of her cheek, thinking about that. "All roads lead you where you're meant to be."

Elliot leaned back on the couch, bringing her with him. "Exactly. I love you. Maybe it is fast, but it's right. I mean, we don't have to start trying right this minute or get married next week. But I want all of it. With you."

Kate's smile started on the inside and spread to her lips. "I want that too. With you and the girls. I want all of it. I love you, Elliot."

He closed his eyes and breathed deeply. "I'm really glad." He opened his eyes and sat up, nudging her off his lap. "The girls seemed pretty sure of what you wanted for Christmas. I figured that if you were at all unsure about us, about everything, maybe this would convince you."

When he stood up, so did Kate, her eyebrows scrunching together. "I'm not unsure. At all. What would convince me?"

"Stay right here," he said.

Kate stood still, refusing to pace or worry about what he was doing. She heard a door again and realized it was the garage. Unable to stay in one spot, she walked to the fireplace and flipped the switch. Orange and yellow flames danced immediately.

The door opened and closed again. She stepped away from the fire, listening but heard nothing. Pacing, she tried to be patient but curiosity won out. She was heading for the kitchen, intent on finding out what he was doing, when Elliot came back into the living room. In his arms, he was holding a wriggling, whining ball of grey fur.

Kate rushed over. "Oh my goodness! You got a puppy?"

Elliot's cheeks scrunched up when the dog licked at him and tried to nip. His little nose sniffed at his shirt. "I got you, *us,* a puppy. She's a Weimaraner. They're smart and good with kids. They have a lot of energy, but I figure the girls will match her there."

Kate stopped in front of him and reached out a hand, then paused. "Wait. You got a puppy hoping I'd stay?"

Elliot shrugged. "Who could leave this face?" He held the puppy up in front of her.

Kate took her from Elliot and snuggled the little one into her chest. "Not me. But I'm pretty fond of your face too. I wasn't planning on leaving it."

Elliot wrapped his arms around Kate, laughing when the dog gave a tiny bark that sounded more like a meow. "That's good news. But the girls were really sure you wanted a puppy. And I want to give you everything I can to make you happy."

The puppy settled her snout on Kate's neck, its breath tickling her skin. "You make me happy, Elliot. You and Beth and Grace. I just want you. I want this. I want us to be a family."

Elliot's eyes darkened as he came closer and kissed her, sinking into her as his hand found its way into her hair. The dog perked up, pushing its nose between them.

They both laughed and Elliot's hand settled at the base of Kate's neck. "We already are. Maybe by next year, we'll be an even bigger one," he said.

The puppy started to yip and squiggle. Kate passed her back. "Let's see how we do with a puppy and two girls first."

Elliot laughed and kissed her again. "Probably a good idea."

They sat on the couch, the puppy between them. Elliot pressed play on the movie and with the fire crackling in the background and Elliot's fingers linked with hers, she wondered if there'd ever been a better Christmas.

"Kate?"

"Hmm?"

"Next Christmas, it'd be nice if all of us shared the same last name."

Kate looked at him, wondering if he could see her heart flailing around in her chest. She leaned in to kiss him, careful not to wake the puppy. "Even the puppy?"

Elliot frowned. "We should probably give her a first name."

Kate's heart continued to hammer like it wanted right out of her chest. They were talking about being married and living happily ever after and all she could think was *"yes."*

"Where were you born?" Kate asked, knowing he'd moved to Angel's Lake for the job.

"Indiana."

Kate thought about it. Played with the word in her mind. "Indy. Indy Peters. I like it. Do you like it?"

With the same care he'd give a newborn, Elliot transferred the pup to the corner of the couch and then turned to Kate.

"I do. It's a good name. You know what other name sounds pretty great?"

Kate grinned, moving closer, her fingers playing with the collar of his shirt. "Hmm."

Yanking her against him, he whispered against her mouth, "Kate Peters. That's a good name."

"Or Elliot Aarons. Also a good name."

Elliot pulled back and laughed. "I might actually like it better. Except then the girls would have to change their names or we wouldn't match."

Kate trailed her lips up the side of his neck up to his ear. "You're right. I guess we better go with yours," she whispered.

She lost her train of thought when his hands started gliding over her body beneath her shirt as his lips met hers over and over again. "Elliot?"

She felt his smile against her neck. "Hmm?"

"I think this is my favorite Christmas ever."

Pulling back, Elliot looked at her like he saw her completely. Like he wanted everything she was or wasn't. Would be or wouldn't. Good or bad. No matter what. *That* was the best gift.

"Next year will be even better," he promised.

Acknowledgements

How to begin? I wrote Kate in June of this year after some fans of Falling for Lucy gently suggested they wanted another visit to Angel's Lake. I was happy to go back. I've always loved small town stories where you care about not just the hero and heroine, but the people who matter to them. Thank you to Jessica at Penner for her constant support and acceptance of my stories. Thank you to my editor, Carolyn for pushing me to make sure every character was represented in the best way possible, regardless of their purpose in the story. Thank you Brenda, Christy, and Tara for taking time from your busy schedules to read this when it was nowhere near Christmas time. Thank you to my family: my husband and my daughters for always supporting my writing and for encouraging it and believing in me when I forget to do that for myself. Thank you to anyone and everyone who reads my stories. Without you, they're just documents on my computer. Thank you for giving them life. Thank you everyone else at Penner, including the cover designer who makes my stories look so appealing at first glance. Thanks to my mom for loving everything I write. I'm forgetting someone, I'm sure, but the good news is, I have four more books coming out, so I can make amends in the next one. Thanks to my twitter peeps for amusing me with both words and gifs. Thank you Kara for always letting me bounce ideas off of you. It's comforting to know you live on the computer like I do. To anyone I forgot, you matter. I'm just forgetful. Merry Christmas everyone. Hope yours is as special as Kate and Elliot's.

About The Author

Jody Holford lives in British Columbia with her husband and two daughters. She's a huge fan of Rainbow Rowell, Nora Roberts, Jill Shalvis, and Emily Giffen. She's unintentionally funny and rarely on time for anything. She loves books, Converse shoes, and diet Pepsi, in no particular order. When she has to go out into the real world, she's a teacher. She writes multiple genres but her favourite is romance because she's a big fan of love and finding happily ever after. Probably because she's lucky enough to have both.

Do you love the Penner Publishing book you've just finished?

Great books deserve great readers.

Please review this book on your favorite retailer, bookish site, blog or on your own social media.

Penner Publishing is a boutique publisher specializing in women driven fiction. We love our romance heroines saucy or sweet. We also love a great story even when there isn't a hot hero involved. It's all about the woman's journey.

Be sure to visit us at:
www.pennerpublishing.com/readers-club
Facebook.com/pennerpub
Twitter.com/pennerpub

Made in the USA
Charleston, SC
05 December 2016